Tim Jones has published two volumes of poetry, a novel, and one earlier collection of short stories. He is a writer, editor, web content manager, husband, father, political activist, and lover of cricket, music, and many other fine things. He lives in Wellington.

Trans*ported*

SHORT STORIES

Tim Jones

V

VINTAGE

creative
nz
ARTS COUNCIL OF NEW ZEALAND *TOI AOTEAROA*

The assistance of Creative New Zealand is greatfully acknowledged by the publishers.

A catalogue record for this book is available from the
National Library of New Zealand

A VINTAGE BOOK

published by
Random House New Zealand
18 Poland Road, Glenfield, Auckland, New Zealand
www.randomhouse.co.nz

Random House International
Random House
20 Vauxhall Bridge Road
London, SW1V 2SA
United Kingdom

Random House Australia (Pty) Ltd
Level 3, 100 Pacific Highway
North Sydney 2060, Australia

Random House South Africa Pty Ltd
Isle of Houghton
Corner Boundary Road and Carse O'Gowrie
Houghton 2198, South Africa

Random House Publishers India Private Ltd
301 World Trade Tower, Hotel Intercontinental Grand Complex
Barakhamba Lane, New Delhi 110 001, India

First published 2008

© 2008 Tim Jones
The moral rights of the author have been asserted

ISBN 978 1 86941 984 4

Random House New Zealand uses non-chlorine-bleached papers from sustainably managed
plantation forests.

Design: Kate Barraclough
Cover illustration: 'Castaway Bardo' by Maryrose Crook
Cover design: Kate Yiakmis
Author photo: Sonali Mukherji
Printed in Australia by Griffin Press

Many of the stories in this collection benefited from comments from members of the various writers' groups I've belonged to. So, with thanks for all the helpful suggestions they have made and the encouragement they have given, I'd like to dedicate this book to the members of the Writers' Intensive Care Group (Dunedin), the Phoenix Writers' SIG (Wellington), and the Writing Crew (Wellington).

CONTENTS

ACKNOWLEDGEMENTS

I'd like to thank publisher Harriet Allan and editor Claire Gummer for their support, expertise and encouragement; the Random House production team for turning the edited manuscript into the book you hold in your hands; and my partner Kay and son Gareth for putting up with my many quirks (not all of which I can blame on being a writer). I would also like to acknowledge the magazines and anthologies that first published a number of the stories in this collection. Bernard Gadd, who passed away recently, edited the anthologies in which my first two published stories appeared: my particular thanks go to him.

The stories listed below have been previously published as follows:
'Rat up a Drainpipe', *Boys' Own Stories: Short Stories by New Zealand Men,* ed. Graeme Lay (Tandem Press, 2000)
'When She Came Walking', *Strange Horizons* (24 September 2001)
'A Short History of the Twentieth Century, with Fries', *Flashquake* Volume 4, Issue 1(Fall 2004)

'Win a Day with Mikhail Gorbachev!', *Full Unit Hookup* (Summer 2002), republished in *Best New Zealand Fiction 4*, ed. Fiona Farrell (Vintage, 2007)

'Sisters', *JAAM* 17 (May, 2002)

'Not Wanted on Voyage', *Bravado* 1 (November 2003)

'Alarm', *Bravado* 5 (November 2005)

'Homestay', *Strange Horizons* (31 January 2005)

'The Visit of M. Foucault to His Brother Wayne', published as 'The Visit', *JAAM* 24 (2006)

'Borges and I', *Winedark Sea* 1 (2000), republished in *Turbine* 1 (October 2001)

'After the War', *Scheherazade* 26 (2004)

'Morning on Volkov', *Nanonights,* ed. Yvonne Eve Walus (Pipers' Ash, 2000)

'The Royal Tour', *JAAM* 24 (2006)

'Queen of the Snows', *100 New Zealand Short Short Stories 4,* ed. Graeme Lay (Tandem Press, 2000)

'Going to the People', published as 'Statesman', *I Have Seen the Future,* ed. Bernard Gadd (Longman Paul, 1986)

'Books in the Trees', *Turbine* (2002).

RAT UP A DRAINPIPE

It was cold down by the harbour in the early morning, and the new chum shivered as he waited for the Parramatta ferry. He found a Thomas Cook's and then a breakfast bar. 'You're a Kiwi, aren't you?' said the woman at the counter. 'Say "fush and chups".'

He wanted a croissant and a coffee, but he said fush and chups for her anyway, and smiled at her witty reply. He took the food outside and sat out of the wind at a little metal table, shading his eyes as the sun winked off the salt cellar. A shadow fell across him. 'Mind if I join you?' asked the shadow, and he pulled his coffee towards him in assent. She was as tall as a tanalised fencepost, as lovely as a jacaranda in spring, with swimmer's shoulders and dancer's hips. Her name was Zoe. His name was Dean.

He didn't see her again till he was on the ferry, watching the finest harbourside real estate in the world slide by. She was with her boyfriend, a stockman from Dubbo way who was taking her back to meet his father, his beautiful but troubled mother, his tall clean-limbed sisters. The stockman knew his sisters would be reserved at first, perhaps even hostile; but as the seasons turned they would warm to Zoe, welcoming her into the family, sharing their most treasured secrets and their tough, practical outdoors clothing. Then the stockman would see that his mother's heart was eased, and ride with his bride across acres turned emerald by love.

Into the head of the harbour flows the Parramatta River, heavy and greasy, slipping by like a raw oyster down a gullet. The ferry nosed up it slowly, the captain keeping a weather eye out for crocodiles that might drag unwary passengers down to a cruel death. Dean was glad when they reached the jetty, and fortified himself with lunch before heading off to the bus station.

It rained all the way to Canberra, and even a stop in Goulburn did little to ease the monotony. Looking at his map as they crested the final rise, he was surprised to see that he was still a long way from the desert.

The people of Australia, embarrassed by their capital, had brushed it under a carpet of trees. By the shores of Lake Burley Griffin he lay down to rest, convinced that the real Canberra was submerged in the lake, its bells still to be heard on clear summer evenings.

A noise woke him. There had been an explosion, and fragments of a building were sailing over the lake. Some landed short, in the water; some overshot him and crashed through the treetops; one found his range. When he came to, he was surrounded by a circle of anxious onlookers going through his wallet for clues.

'Mate, he's a Kiwi!'

A weatherbeaten face, bending towards him. 'Mate, are you okay? Can you say "fush and chups"? Mate?' He closed his eyes and slipped away.

Leaf-dappled sunlight slanted through the hospital windows. He lay back and listened to the conversations of the policy advisers and archivists who occupied the neighbouring beds. They said George Gregan and a few of the blokes from the ACT Brumbies were visiting the kids' ward tomorrow to cheer the little buggers up. I could do with cheering up, he thought, and asked the nurse to bring him some books. He read *The Fatal Shore*, *The Songlines*, and *For the Term of His Natural Life*. They were all about Australia.

The spell in hospital blew out the schedule a bit, and there were some problems with the travel insurance. When they released him, he lit out north by west, hitching rides on road trains and cattle trucks, eking out his remaining funds on sausages and chips, egg and chips, sausages egg and chips. He grew bloated with grease and inanition.

'You're a Kiwi?' asked his latest truckdriver. He nodded, dreading what was to come.

'You'd know all about the GST, then?'

Twenty minutes later, he had found his station in life. He got the driver to drop him off at a farmers' pub in

Parkes, bought a bloke a beer, and started asking around. He spent that evening sorting out five boxes of receipts, invoices, docking rings, dockets, odd bits of wire and stock feed catalogues. By 2am he had separated out everything that wasn't directly relevant, and after a few hours' sleep he was hard at work again, with calculator in one hand and the Australian Tax Office's chirpy *The GST and You* booklet in the other. It took a few calls to the Tax Reform Infoline, where All Our Operators were often Attending To Other Clients, but as the family settled for dinner around the big communal table he ticked the last box, totalled the last totals, and received their awestruck thanks.

He spent several weeks in the district, moving from one farm to another, till one night a few blokes from a local accounting firm cornered him in the pub and explained, with the aid of two broken bottles and a chair leg, that they had been suffering a business downturn that might be attributable to his activities. They recommended that he be out of Parkes by sun-up.

Nothing daunted, he hit the road again, working his way up to Dubbo through the foothills of the mountains. The accounting life was good to him; all the lifting boxes and totting up columns of figures were doing wonders for his muscles, and the weeks on the road were giving him a tan and the weatherbeaten complexion of a man who'd seen much but wasn't telling.

He saw Zoe while he was trying out a new Akubra. She had come into town with the boyfriend's sisters, but he could see at once that it hadn't gone to plan, that the hidden depths she had hoped to plumb in her boyfriend were drained and empty, that the family was close-mouthed and suspicious. The boyfriend's mother had all but accused her of wanting to marry into the family's money and fritter it away on new dresses and DVDs. Yet, without really meaning to, she had moved from girlfriend to fiancée, and now they were all getting at her: name a date, name a date, why don't you name a date?

He trailed around behind them until the conversation turned to the GST — 'If we don't have to pay it on food, why should we have to pay it on clothes?', then walked up, as casual as you please, and said he was a Kiwi, and could he help? It was simplicity itself to move from the GST on clothing to GST in general, from GST in general to the state of the farm's accounts in particular, to make the happy discovery that she had taken on responsibility for them, to offer his help and have it accepted.

Perhaps he meant to have it go no further than that. It began as a strictly commercial relationship, terms strictly cash, and during accounts receivables, petty cash, and reconciliations, they kept to business. But something in the melancholy business of depreciation must have touched her soul, for she threw down her personal organiser, turned to him with a shudder, and said, 'I can't go on.'

'Weary eyes?'

'A weary heart.'

Dean's heart became a barque adrift on the flood of her tears. Then they made love atop a shifting pile of old bank statements, after which they rattled through the depreciation in no time.

Stolen moments: a dilapidated hut at the far end of the property, the back of the ute after a quick trip to town. The accounts had been in a mess, but there was a limit to how long the recovery process could be drawn out, and he was getting some odd looks from the boyfriend.

'I'll be leaving on Saturday, then,' he told them, having told her in private.

'Tell you what, mate,' said the patriarch, pressing a cold one into his hand, 'why not stay till Sunday? We're a man short for the cricket team. Do you bat or bowl?'

He suggested Zoe could do it instead, but was told this was serious stuff: there was no room for sheilas in country cricket. What the hell, he thought. One more chance to stick it to these Aussies.

Things weren't looking too good when he came in. Four for 38, chasing 247. He'd bowled a few overs of his nondescript medium pace and even picked up a wicket, but he hoped his batting wasn't as rusty as his bowling. His partner was Zoe's fiancé, who played like he made love, if what Zoe told him was true. 'You just run the singles, mate, and I'll do the slogging,' he was told when he came to the wicket.

For a time, it worked well. They put on ten, then twenty, then fifty, of which he had eight. He had got used to the sledging by now — 'Say fush and chups, ya Kiwi barstard!' — and was even making limited eye contact with his batting partner. Then it happened: a push to mid-on, clearly no run there; looking up to see his partner halfway down the wicket; a cry of 'No'; the bails whipped off before his partner could regain his ground.

'Sorry, mate!'

No reply.

He was out shortly afterwards — a tired shot to a ball he should have left alone — and there was a stony silence when he returned to the pavilion. When he went for a piss, they were waiting for him. Evidently Zoe had been confiding in some girl she knew, whose boyfriend was the team's wicketkeeper — and wicketkeepers talk all day, and all night too.

After they beat the shit out of him, they slung his bag in the dust and told him to pick it up and start walking. He limped away till he was out of sight, then doubled back and borrowed the farm ute, leaving the keys in the ignition — this was the country, after all. He drove to the medical centre in town, said he'd had a fall. 'Funny sort of fall,' the doctor said, but didn't take it further. Nothing was broken.

Zoe had pleaded a headache and stayed behind at the farm. He left the ute behind a tree and walked the last kilometre, found her in the kitchen, said he'd be moving on, said goodbye for good. Then he felt like a drongo, and told her he loved her, and maybe if he got back to Kiwiland he'd send her a card, and she should always remember GST didn't apply to exports. They smiled, remembering, then she said she'd had enough of this shitty family and this shitty town and if she was ready in five minutes could he drive her to the bus depot? So the last he saw of her was a wave from the window of a bus bound for Sydney.

He didn't want the cops after him, so he parked the ute outside Grace Bros, dropped the keys off at the lost property office, and set off walking. He took only roads going inland, and within a week he had passed through Broken Hill, crossed the Barrier Range, and reached the edge of the desert. As he walked on, the sun drove the words from his head, so that he saw only shapes, angles, and shadows, and had no idea what they meant. At night, the words returned, and with them the hope that some tribe would take him up and initiate him into their secrets, so that he could move through this land with the ease and confidence that had always eluded him in his own. He had been wondering where the first people were ever since he arrived, but he was no closer to knowing.

It was very cold at night, and very hot in the day. One day, near noon, he stumbled and fell into a shallow gully. As the sun westered, the rim of the gully shaded him, and he revived. There was water there, just under the earth; he drank it and staggered to his feet.

He was feeling hungry by the time he reached the road, but there was no food in his pack or pockets. He was contemplating what to do about this when two blokes in a Kingswood told him to hop in.

'Jim,' said Jim, and Don said, 'Don.'

'Mates, gidday.' His command of language had returned as soon as he climbed in the car.

'Jeez, mate,' said Jim, 'you look a bit knackered. Want a drink?'

'Thanks, mate.' He drank deep, and then followed their example and tossed the can out the window, where, over millennia, it decomposed and added its minerals to the thin soil. Long before then, of course, the dregs of the beer had dried and been carried off by ants. Nothing is wasted in the end.

SAID SHEREE

Sheree and Miranda met at a party. Each left with the other on her mind.

Several weeks later, the Mexican Ambassador, a keen patron of the arts, held a reception. Miranda, ranked as a Tier Two poet for funding purposes, saw Sheree across the room. Miranda made a beeline for her — only to realise that Sheree was with a group of Tier Ones. Embarrassed, Miranda backed away.

That would have been that; but, a little to the north and far beneath their feet, Gaia shifted in her sleep. Poets and patrons alike rushed for doorways and crush-proof spaces. Sheree and Miranda found themselves pressed together against an antimacassar. Their mutual awkwardness was obliterated by fear. 'You're beautiful,' said Sheree. Miranda, plain and tall, was swept away.

Heads were counted once the tremor passed and

the tumult subsided. Miranda and Sheree were missing. Separately, from Sheree's bed, they phoned in their excuses.

Miranda went home. 'I haven't seen you for days,' her flatmate remarked. It wasn't much of a flat, not really, and the flatmate held the lease.

'You can move in with me,' said Sheree.

Having lugged the last of her boxes up Sheree's steps, Miranda went out on the deck. The harbour view, which she had admired since the first night she spent there, now felt like hers. The weather was grey and cold. Far below, hardy ants, gloved and muffled, scurried to and fro on the beach.

Between Miranda's job and Sheree's funding, they had enough to pay the rent, and a little left over. They each had time to write. Sheree wrote in the morning, after Miranda had left for work, and spent the afternoon completing grant applications and working on a project to deliver sonnets by mobile phone. Some platform-specific issues were still to be resolved.

Miranda wrote on Saturday afternoons, while Sheree played hockey.

They had other interests in common. They both collected earthenware. They both loved tramping. In summer, they joined a party heading south to Nelson Lakes. They were the only writers. It was bliss.

They dealt with literary functions by arriving separately and avoiding each other, though they exchanged sly glances when they thought no one was looking.

It worked for a while. But, inevitably, word got around. A small independent publisher agreed to bring out Miranda's first collection. 'I want to be with you at the launch,' said Sheree. 'I'm not going to pretend.'

The publisher had hired a church hall. A few bankable names came along. When Miranda read, Sheree stood in the front row. When Miranda signed, Sheree sat next to her. 'You must be so proud of her,' someone told Sheree.

Sheree's third collection was launched at Unity. Sheree dragged Miranda along. That didn't go so well. Miranda hung back, feeling like a fraud. Sheree talked with her friends and cast irritated glances Miranda's way.

Miranda retreated to the outer shelves, looking at an omnibus edition of Ursula Bethell. Blanche Baughan was reassuringly close at hand.

Sheree forgave her. They forgave each other. They got drunk. They compared royalty statements. 'It's more about grants and residencies,' explained Sheree.

In the autumn, Miranda was up for reclassification. Without the support of a university press, Miranda had no realistic hope of moving up to Tier One, but she was still disappointed when the envelope came.

'Never mind,' said Sheree. 'I love you anyway.'

Sheree's status was secure for two more years.

Miranda came home from work a few weeks later to find Sheree bouncing off the walls. 'Look at this!' she said.

It was an invitation from the northern festival circuit: Nuuk and Norilsk, Vorkuta, Longyearbyen. Four weeks

north of the Arctic Circle, reading, writing, workshopping.
And watching out for polar bears — they could kill you.
'I'm to be preceded by a man with a rifle,' said Sheree.

New Zealand literature had never before been
represented so far north. It was a feather in everyone's cap.

'I'll miss you so much,' said Miranda. She clung to
Sheree, tenderly, fiercely.

Sheree bought Miranda a video-enabled phone before
she left. Four weeks of Sheree — blonde hair poking out
of her fur-lined hood — cavorting with new friends,
silhouetted against snow, standing next to oil drums full
of burning blubber to keep warm.

Nuuk, the capital of Greenland, was surprisingly
cosmopolitan. Norilsk was one giant chemical dump.
In Vorkuta, Sheree won the V. I. Morozov Prize for Best
Recital of an Individual Work, for her declamatory piece
in the style of Gregory Corso. The prize, thanks to a well-
connected local businessman, was paid in US dollars. With
the news, Sheree sent an air ticket. 'I'm stopping over in
the Caribbean on the way home to thaw out,' said Sheree.
'See you in Basseterre!'

It took some nerve to ask, but Miranda's boss was
understanding. 'I wish I could go with you,' Miranda's
boss said, and Miranda realised, suddenly, that she
meant it.

Basseterre! Miranda had never heard of it. Palms
shaded the beach, the locals talked about cricket, and
once they had circumnavigated the island of St Kitts,
there was nothing to do but eat, drink, sleep, and make

love. Sheree kept Miranda entertained with tales from the frozen north. Longyearbyen had been the wildest of the lot. 'Those Norwegians!' said Sheree. They were crazy up there on Spitsbergen. So were the bears.

They came home to the wind and the rain. Sheree set to work completing her fourth collection and editing podcasts from the festivals. She had secured funding for a G5 workstation, her latest pride and joy. Miranda had three poems published in *Takahe* and two more accepted by *JAAM*. She read at the Angus Inn. It was a wet night in the Hutt Valley, and some of the locals stayed away. Her collection, which was now heavily discounted, sold three copies. Not bad, considering. She was given a voucher for petrol, though she had conscientiously taken the train.

Sheree's poem about their week together in the Caribbean became justly famous and has been much anthologised.

Miranda's boss gave her a promotion. Miranda and Sheree joined a soccer team. Sheree was the centre forward. Miranda was a holding midfielder.

Delivering sonnets by mobile phone had not been a complete success, but the project hit the jackpot with haiku. Haiku were back, said Sheree.

People grow and change. It's nothing to be ashamed of. A new funding category, Tier Four, was introduced. In consequence, Tier Two poets became eligible to be mentors, and Miranda took on a mentee. She was young, tiny, a wounded bird. Her name was Caroline. She lived in Johnsonville.

Nothing might have come of it, had Sheree's success at Vorkuta not been noticed in high places. It took a public–private partnership, with a mixture of tagged funding, corporate sponsorship in three bands, and matching government contributions, but at last the deal could be announced. Sheree would be New Zealand's first poet in space! She would carry leading New Zealand brands to low earth orbit, and return with a three-book deal.

It was on for young and old. Sheree became public property, meeting the Prime Minister, appearing on *Takatāpui* and *Kiwifruit*. In months, in weeks, in days, she was off to Star City to train for her mission.

'I love you,' she told Miranda, from the airport, from Moscow, from Star City. Photos: Sheree in a centrifuge, her compact body whirling round. Sheree hanging weightless in the hydrolab. The two cosmonauts who would be flying her to the International Space Station, Valentina and Vsevolod. Their brave little Soyuz spacecraft. I love you, Miranda, said Sheree.

Miranda's mentee was promising but needy. Miranda allowed herself to engage in conduct that was inappropriate to the mentor–mentee relationship and breached the terms of her contract with the funding agency. She reproached herself late at night, as she watched Caroline sleeping.

Sheree appeared on BBC World, CNN, and Al Arabiya.

Miranda kept writing. A second published collection would be something. Not everyone made it that far.

Live streaming video of the launch, with Russian-language commentary, was available. Using high-speed broadband on Sheree's G5, Miranda was able to hear the countdown, see the rocket on the launch pad, watch it vault upwards into space.

Sheree made contact. Docking had been successful, and she was aboard the space station. Three months to do nothing but write, and sleep, and float. (And help around the place; tidiness was especially important in space.) Every ninety-two minutes, she would pass overhead.

The mentoring period finished. Caroline could now be revealed as Miranda's girlfriend. She had dependency issues, but that meant she was usually home.

Miranda broke the news to Sheree by scheduled uplink. Sheree did not respond immediately. One orbit passed, two. Then Sheree said she was sad, but not surprised. Also, two nights ago, she and Valentina . . .

Miranda had three poems published in *Bravado*. *Sport* and *Landfall* regretted to inform. *Trout* did not reply.

As a result of Miranda's excellent mentoring, Caroline was reclassified to Tier Three. She sold a poem to *North & South*. You're going places, girl, thought Miranda.

Caroline had an empty room and a double bed. Miranda decided she was going places too. She moved her boxes out of Sheree's house, down the steps, and off to Johnsonville. She promised Sheree that she'd continue to water her plants. Sheree had already asked Miranda and Caroline to come for dinner the first weekend after she got home from Russia. I want to be your best friend, said Sheree.

When the last lot of boxes was safely in Caroline's van, Miranda returned to stand on the balcony for one last look across the harbour. Oh, she would miss the view! On the promenade below, hardy ants rode skateboards, walked dogs, and ate products containing dairy, gluten, and traces of nuts.

Above, the stars shone steadily. Among them was Sheree. Miranda could see her clearly. She was looking out of a porthole, smiling fondly down.

WHEN SHE CAME WALKING

The first time she walked down our street, pots jumped off stoves, coal leapt from scuttles, wood went rat-a-tat-tatting down hallways. In our yard, a broom and spade got up and lurched around like drunks, trying to decide which way she'd gone.

I caught my first glimpse of her from the window, and that was enough for me. 'I'll be back soon,' I told Mother, and slipped out the door before the questions could start. It was all I could do to stop the door coming with me, and the street looked like a parade had passed through: everything from Mrs Ormond's wrought-iron railing to Connor O'Brien's henhouse had torn free of its moorings and sashayed down the street after her. Lacking much in the way of legs, the henhouse hadn't got far, but there were frightened hens clucking about and eggs lying hither and yon.

I left Mr O'Brien to sort them out and followed Mrs Ormond and her railing. She was cursing it a blue streak and telling it to get the hell back to where it came from, but it wasn't paying any attention. It clumped down the road on its six metal legs, making a fair speed and leaving her in its wake. Damn, I thought, damn, I'm going to have to stop and help her. Why didn't she fix the damn thing securely in the ground?

I ran after the railing and caught it with one hand as it was turning into Fenton Avenue — and Fenton Avenue was so full of writhing inanimate objects I was happy the railing was there to delay me. 'Come here, you,' I said, and concentrated on it as best I could. Gradually, the railing's struggles eased to a few hopeful twitches. I could barely keep it upright, and I was glad when Mrs Ormond's strong hands came to join mine.

'Thanks, Pat, you're a pal. Help me get this back home, and there's sure to be some cookies and a drink at the end of it.'

I wanted to remind her I wasn't eight any more, but there was no changing some people. 'Give them to Ma for me, would you? I was headed the other way.'

She shook her head. 'If you take my advice, you'll go home and stay there — but there's no chance of that, I suppose.'

'None at all,' I told her.

By the time we had wrestled the railing back to Mrs Ormond's yard, it had given up its dreams of freedom, and it lay down meekly at the foot of her steps. 'Now would you care to fetch Carl Dooley for me, Pat?'

I was already backing away up the street. 'I think you'll find Carl's got his hands full today,' I told her. 'Almond cookies! I'll be back for them!'

Fenton Avenue was full of irate householders, Harvest Lane likewise, and why in the name of the Lord had she chosen to walk through the market? Fruit and vegetables still counted as alive, but empty crates and wooden trestles evidently didn't, where she was concerned. There was real anger here, and calls for vengeance. I began to think Mrs Ormond might have a point, but I hadn't come this far to give up now. I dodged a box, parried a table, and went on.

It was like walking into a fog. One moment, bustle, cries of alarm, the whicker of wood flying end over end; the next, only my footfalls broke the silence.

Then I saw her. The police had encircled her, and all I could see was a glimpse of tousled hair. Half of them were facing her, half facing outwards, frowns of concentration on their brows. What the police lack in power, they make up for in determination, and nothing was moving on this section of the street that didn't have two legs and a legitimate reason.

The legs they could see, and I was working on the legitimate reason as I walked towards her, no more able to resist than the wrought-iron railing.

Next to a police station is the best location in town, and the shops here sold stuff we'd never be able to afford, and dared to keep it behind glass. I veered away from the cops and pretended to look at some furniture while watching the reflected scene behind me. One of the cops was giving me a mighty fierce glare — that, or he was simply trying to stop the glass from breaking.

They were trying to persuade her to come to the station, and she begged to differ. One of the cops lost patience and grabbed her arm. I saw his wooden baton waggle its way free from his belt, float up beside him, and tap him smartly on the head.

That did it. The outward-facing cops turned inwards, and in a moment the street came to life. I ducked and rolled as a shower of glass exploded above my head and a procession of heavy chairs, ornate tables, and long couches made for sinning waddled onto the roadway. The cops and their quarry were moving in a tight little group towards the doors of the police station, currently the only safe place in the neighbourhood. I ran towards them, ducked between two blue-clad bodies, and found myself face to face with her.

'You! Out of here!'

'Sorry, sir, I was passing, the street went nuts, nearly lost my head, safest place I could find . . .'

'He was looking in that window just before it blew out!'

'Another one, eh?' An arm descended on my shoulders, and I was hauled inside the building with her. The doors shut behind us and the din ended.

'I'm Patrick,' I said. 'Pleased to meet you.'

'No talking, you!'

So I just grinned. She stopped looking worried long enough to grin back.

How can I tell you how lovely she looked at that moment? She was a head shorter than me, blonde-haired — a rare sight indeed in this town — dishevelled, careworn. I wanted to wrap her in my warmest coat and take her home for soup and Mrs Ormond's almond cookies.

That didn't appear likely any time soon. We were put in separate but adjoining cells, locked, guarded, inert. When I tried to talk to the guard, he snarled, 'Shut up!'

For the first time, I felt afraid. 'We'll be out of here soon,' I told her.

'I hope so,' she said. Then she burst into tears.

I reached through the bars to pat her on the shoulder, but the guard growled, 'Stop that, you!' I took a hasty step backwards and waited for the tears to stop. In a way, I was pleased she was crying, because it meant I could afford a few sniffles myself.

When she'd calmed a little, she looked at me and said, 'Sorry.'

'No need. I'm scared too.'

'I dragged you into all this . . .'

'No you didn't! My mother always said curiosity would be the death of me. I had to find out what was causing such an uproar in our street.'

She looked even gloomier. 'Did I cause a lot of damage?'

'Anything that was damaged should have been tied down better,' I said gallantly. 'But couldn't you have made your way through town a bit more quietly?'

'I was trying to! I come from the country, and I'm not used to great cities like this. I was all right till I started looking around and thinking how grand everything was —'

Grand? Our neighbourhood?

'— and then I noticed things following me, and I got scared and ran, and that made it worse.'

'And the policeman's baton?'

'They had no cause treating me as a criminal!' The bars of her cage flexed a little.

'Enough talking!' barked the guard.

'How long are you going to hold us here?' I countered. 'We have rights, you know.'

'A professor from the college is coming for her. I don't know about you.'

'Can I get a message to my mother, then? She'll be worried sick.'

'Should have thought of that earlier.'

'I know I'm allowed one message.'

Pad and pen produced from pocket. 'Here. Fifty words maximum.'

I was on my third sheet of paper, still trying to phrase things the right way, when a bustle of officialdom arrived. The man at its centre addressed my beloved severely.

'Miss Quigley, I have had to make some very detailed explanations to arrange your release. Substantial reparations have been demanded. In this instance, the value of your unique capacities to our research programme has persuaded the chancellor to pay them in full. Any repetition of this incident will not be tolerated. Captain, if you would be so kind?'

A flourish of keys. She whispered, 'Good luck!' as they led her away.

'Hey, what about me?' I called. 'I'm the innocent victim of forces I don't understand!'

The professorial type focused on me for a moment. 'Then study, young man. You must take responsibility for your own destiny.'

The captain was holding the door open for him. They had forgotten me before it closed.

Crumple sheet three, start sheet four. 'Dear Mother, I know this will come as a shock to you . . .'

They didn't believe me at first. When I started to bring home books, they said I would never read them. When they found me asleep over Mundine's *Principles*, they woke me and said it was time to cut the firewood — not a job for the absent-minded. When I passed the preliminary entrance test, there might have been a brief mutter of congratulations, but then they went back to the big news of the day: Mrs Ormond and Carl Dooley were to be married, and the late Mr Ormond not yet a year in his grave! 'There was a power of ironmongery in that house even while Mr Ormond still drew breath,' said Mother darkly, but my sisters were already picking out their dresses.

When I told them I would be sitting the final entrance test in four weeks' time, and asked to be relieved of household duties till then, my father took me aside for a talking. The last time that happened, I had been ten, scared and sullen, locked in the storeroom of the greengrocer for filching his oranges. The fear of my father's belt had hung over the whole encounter, though he never used it.

Well, I was eighteen now, too big and too fast to be hit, whatever my mother might say. He took me through to the parlour, reserved for receiving the priest, the landlord, and our Saviour should he chance to drop by. Lately, I'd been using it as a quiet place to study.

'Your mother had you marked out for the priesthood,' he began, 'and now you do this to us.'

This was feeble, and he knew it. 'The Lord has other plans for me,' I said.

'Why engineering, then? Nothing good ever came of it.'

'It was a noble profession once, Father. I want to make it noble again.'

'Noble, is it? Then how do you explain that terrible business with the nave of St Dominic's, or those hare-brained gas lamps, or that Mr Deutschendorf and his 'suspension bridge'? And he was a professor at this very college you insist on attending!'

'Ah, but that's the point, Father. Those projects failed because they were designed for yesterday's conditions. When you were a boy, did things move around as much as they do now?'

'No,' he allowed, 'they generally stayed where they were.'

'Exactly! And that's because there weren't so many of

us then, and we lived in villages, not in cities. As long as they didn't come under focused attack, even flimsy structures were perfectly safe. But now there's so many of us that any concentration of thoughts can send iron and stone and even wood breaking free and wandering away.' That Miss Quigley could do all this and more on her own, I kept to myself.

'Meaning I have to pay good money to you and your sisters to think our house into shape.'

I privately disputed his definition of 'good money', but now wasn't the time to argue the point. He was rising to my lure.

'That's right. So what are we going to do? Go back to living in thatch and wattle?'

He made a face at that.

'This is the old way, Dad' — I held up Mundine's *Principles* — 'and this is the new way' — Lyman and Parker's *Engineering in the Age of Uncertainty*. 'I want to make the new way work.'

'And how much do you suppose I'll have to pay for all this?'

'Not much at all!' I answered gaily. And then we got down to business.

I passed the final entrance test with a mark or two to spare, and between Father and Mother and Auntie Eileen, who'd always doted on me, my family came up with the money for the first year. 'You'll have to engineer yourself a job after that,' they said.

Inside those imposing walls, the college was unimpressive: a warren of low, flat, narrow-windowed buildings. 'It doesn't pay to build high around students,' I was told.

The first term was torture, a crash course in mathematics and physics and chemistry. Did I really need to know the melting point of sulphur or the value of the Dietrich coefficient? Well, the latter was used in the calculation of animate field flux in inorganic materials, so I guess I did at that.

In between my studies, my duties at home, and my occasional opportunities to escape for a pint and a chat with my fellow students, I tried to find Miss Quigley, which was still the only name I knew her by. She looked no older than me, so I expected to find her somewhere among the junior classes, but nobody knew anything of her. I glimpsed a couple of women with blonde hair, but both were Saxon exchange students who didn't spare me a second glance.

It was a week before the end of term, and I was struggling with Professor Carr's theories about magnetism, when I saw her: just a glimpse, hurrying out of one building and into another, with a couple of burly men by her side. I followed, and was met at the door by one of the men, who pointed to the sign that said NO ADMITTANCE.

'That girl went in,' I said.

'EXCEPT ON OFFICIAL BUSINESS,' he added.

There was plainly no budging him. An exhaustive study of the timetable showed there were no teaching rooms in that building, yet neither was it listed as a research facility. All the windows were locked, all the doors boarded over.

So what about the building she had come from? That was a bit more promising: it contained dormitories for women from country areas and foreign parts who were attending the college. I knew a man who boasted considerable knowledge of such women.

Dan Travis was as thin as a rake and acted accordingly. He claimed to be a magnet to the ladies, and if even half his stories were true, he was right. There had to be some explanation for how a man could eat so much and stay so thin. I bought him lunch and got him talking about the charms of girls from Saxony.

'By then I knew she wanted it, so . . .' Yes, yes, Dan. Spare me the detailed description and concentrate on the interesting bit: how you got into her room.

Oh. You didn't make it back to her room. There was an alleyway. How romantic.

But Dan wasn't done with this flaxen-haired goddess, and eventually his urges drove him to test the fearsome security of the women's dorms.

'And do you know, I just walked right in? And there she was, waiting for me, with her legs—'

'You just walked right in?'

'That's right! These are big girls, after all' — I leered on cue — 'and what they do after hours is their business.'

Let me make it clear at once that what happened next wasn't my fault. I was shaking like Mrs Ormond's railing at the prospect of actually going in there and looking for

Miss Quigley, and even worse, talking to her if I found her, so I spent a couple of hours in the pub watching my classmates play silly games with the tables. By the time I lurched to my feet, squared my shoulders, and set off, I had thrown a skinful of bravado over the black pit of anxiety.

As Dan had said, getting into the dormitory involved nothing more than knocking on the door. I was taken straight to her room, but she wasn't there. Margrethe, one of her room-mates, was.

'With a boyfriend no doubt Kate is outing,' she told me. God forbid Margrethe was any acquaintance of Dan's, for she looked me up and down and said I was a fine-looking fellow, and why didn't I tell her all my troublings? Which I did.

Now, *dormitory* wasn't really the word. The women slept four to a room, but they had an arrangement that ensured a gentleman caller could be entertained in private. And I was here to see Kate — a much sweeter sound than Miss Quigley — but she was out with her boyfriend, damn him for all eternity, and Margrethe was friendly, and warm, and sitting on her bed with her arm brushing mine.

And I found that when I leaned over and kissed her she put her arms around me, and we sank back on the bed, and her flesh was like cream, cool and deep. I came in seconds, then I came in minutes, then we both came in what felt like hours.

'Room-mates coming back to roomen will,' she told me in her endearingly mangled English. I kissed her deeply, found something to wipe myself, pulled on my clothes — God, did I need a shower — kissed her again, and stumbled towards the door.

To be met by Kate Quigley, coming the other way, with no sign of the alleged boyfriend. She raised an eyebrow, smiled, and said, 'I see you've met Margrethe.'

'I . . . er . . .' I said, and fled down the hallway, pursued by the faint sound of laughter. I had a good idea what they were laughing about. It comes of having sisters.

Until I had my brain-wave, my three years of study had been a disillusioning experience. When I walked through the college gates for the first time, I had had two great desires: to find Kate, and to find a way to build the great, airy structures I saw in my mind's eye. I found Kate, or rather she found me; that was my fortune and misfortune both. And all my study had put paid to those idle dreams of construction.

Why are our cities built of wood, not stone? Because stone, never having been alive, has no resistance to the press of our thoughts, and one stone jogged out of place can cause a whole building to come tumbling down. Build in stone, and you need to employ a small army just to think your building firmly in place. Build in wood, and as long as you're not subjected to a concerted attack, or some freak of nature walking by, you will probably be all right. And yet our winters are cold, and the fire bell peals like the crack of doom across our cities.

There are other materials too, iron and that sludgy

stuff they call concrete, and all of them equally vulnerable. Do you know that an optimistic son of the Rhineland has invented an engine that burns oil and can power a carriage without need of horses? Imagine what our cities would be like if they didn't stink of horse shit! We would go zipping about the place in Herr Kessler's invention, smelling the sweet, clean air.

But all it takes is one stray thought, and the whole complicated contraption falls apart, and the oil leaks out and collects in a little puddle on the ground. And the same goes for Mrs Magill and her electric light, and the unfortunate Mr Stephens and his speaking device. (Unfortunate for me, too — I could have used it to call my lovely Margrethe in Saxony and ask how she and her baron were getting along. It had broken my heart to see her go, and other parts of me were just as downcast.)

So we knew what we needed: something with the strength of iron but the stability of living wood. I thought of the answer five minutes from the end of Professor Sullivan's 9am lecture.

I was lucky to be there at all. At 1am, I'd been stumbling home after a hard night's drinking at the Flying Jug. My feet got confused as I walked beside the pond, and before I knew it I was covered in pond scum and fending off the attentions of a duck.

After a long wash and a short sleep, I got up early to avoid explaining the state of my clothing to Mother. In any case, I tried hard not to miss Professor Sullivan's lectures. She was always genuinely interested in what her students had to say, and I was always genuinely interested in talking.

Today's lecture topic was energy barriers to chemical reactions. As far as I'm concerned, chemistry is physics minus the excitement, and I listened with less than my usual attention.

'I can see by the glazed looks on your faces you've all been finding this deeply absorbing,' she announced with a few minutes to go, 'so instead I'll bore you with some of my current research. Professor Koch and I are about to announce in *Chemical Review Letters* that we've invented a new field of chemistry.'

'Do we need a new field of chemistry?' I called out.

She assumed a severe expression. 'Even you might find this interesting, Mr McCreedy. I recall you telling us about Herr Kessler and his carriage that burns oil. That never amounted to much, but we've discovered that oil has other properties of great interest.' She explained how she and Professor Koch had derived carbon compounds from oil and used them to make light, flexible materials with considerable resistance to directed thought. 'They'd be perfect for cups and plates, and even chairs and tables,' she went on, 'but they're not strong enough to build with. We're working on a way to make the stuff into fibres and cables, but we need to increase its resistance to thought as well.'

'I've got an idea,' I told Professor Sullivan as we left the lecture room. 'Have you got five minutes?'

Fifteen minutes later, I had been added to her research

team. Almost a year after that, we were ready to put my brain-wave to the test.

A team of us gathered round a thin coil of material. On the outside was a kind of hardened, transparent resin, and on the inside was a thin filament of carbon (made by controlled pyrolysis of cellulose in an inert atmosphere, if you really want to know). One fibre couldn't take much load, but put a bundle of them together and you had something much lighter and far stronger than iron, ready to build bridges, and vessels, and cables. But, of course, little more immune to the college's Chief Materials Tester than a freestanding iron railing or an incautious policeman's baton. Which was where my idea came in: between the resin and the carbon was a thin film of water, and in that water thrived microscopic pond algae, which in their mindless aliveness would, so we hoped, turn away the most destructive of thoughts.

The Chief Materials Tester walked in. I didn't think she would hold anything back in the testing. Kate and I had exchanged polite conversation once or twice while I'd been waiting for Margrethe. Since Margrethe had departed for her ancestral halls, clutching her degree with one hand and giving me a final squeeze with the other, Kate and I had not exchanged a word.

'Straighten the coil out, please,' she said, and we did. She and her assistant attached instruments, one at each end, one in the middle, and then she stood back a few paces, frowned in concentration, and looked at our handiwork.

Looked at it hard. I could see the lines of strain on her

face. It mirrored my face as I looked at her. Time stretched taut in the room.

And nothing happened. The fibre didn't budge, the needles didn't move. There was a poker in the grate. Kate turned her gaze on it, and it leapt from its place and flew up the chimney. For all I know, it's still climbing. Then she relaxed, stepped back, and said, 'You win.'

Big grins, slaps on the back, time to bundle up the material — we call it carbon fibre — and take it back to the lab. Professor Sullivan was talking to me about further work we needed to do: manufacturing techniques, the micro-pumping problem . . . but I excused myself and asked Kate if she would have dinner with me that night. She said she would.

Kate had moved out of the dormitory and was now boarding privately, and there was a suspicious old biddy standing behind her as she opened the door to me. 'Mind you don't stay out too late, now — I've seen his type before!' the old biddy cautioned. They do say age lends perspective.

Dinner was undoubtedly delicious, but it might have been boiled cardboard for all the attention I paid to it. I was too busy watching Kate. She was wearing something dark and flowing that set off her hair and her beautiful soft skin, and just before her dress got in the way there was a hint of the cleft between her breasts. I wanted so much to slip my finger in there and start undoing the buttons, but I didn't have the nerve. There was coffee, conversation, and dessert — she could pack the food away for such a slim thing, which my mother says is always a good sign. I excused myself to go to the toilet, and while I was sitting there I made up my mind.

'Would you like to come home with me?' I whispered as we stood together outside the restaurant door.

And she thought it over, and said yes, she would like that very much. Our first night was glorious, and our wedding night better still. Each morning we walk to the college together, and each evening we walk back to the room we share in my parents' house. I love my parents, but it's time Kate and I found a place of our own. There's times she and I set the whole house to shaking.

A SHORT HISTORY OF THE TWENTIETH CENTURY, WITH FRIES

By the time they got to the Finland Station, Lenin and his posse were famished.

'What'll it be, boss, Burger King or McDonald's?' asked Zinoviev.

Lenin rustled up the kopecks for a quarter-pounder and fries all round and they set to chowing down. By the time he finished, Lenin had had a better idea.

'I'm tired of this revolution business,' he said. 'Let's set up a chain of family restaurants instead.'

It took a while to convince the Mensheviks, Left SRs, and other petit-bourgeois elements. Nevertheless, Lenin's will prevailed, and Party cadres fanned out across the land in a sophisticated franchising operation. By the end of 1917, Moscow and Petrograd were under complete control, and Siberia was falling into line. Lenin's Bolshevik brand — 'the burger for the worker' — was taking command.

The big international chains didn't take this lying down. With an aggressive combination of discounting, free giveaways, and sheer intimidation, they muscled in on the Bolsheviks. For four years, the struggle went on. The starving inhabitants of Northern Russia woke up each morning not knowing whether the Golden Arches or the Hammer and Sickle would be standing atop their local fast food outlet.

It was a bad time all round, but at the end of it, the red flag with the yellow emblem reigned supreme across Russia. Crowds flocked to enjoy the cheery, efficient service and chomp their way through the basic Bolshevik burger or such additional menu choices as the Red Square (prime Polish beef in a square bun) and the Bronze Horseman (horse testicles on rye — an acquired taste). Fuelled by Bolshevik burgers, Russia was on the move. Tractor production went up twenty per cent. Electricity output doubled in five years.

After Lenin choked to death on a fishburger on 1924, new CEO Joseph Stalin launched a full-scale campaign of collectivisation and industrialisation. Horse testicles were out, borscht was in. These changes were far from universally popular, but, as the slogan went, 'You can't say no to Uncle Joe'. From Murmansk to Magadan, it was Joe's way or the highway.

The years 1939 to 1945 were bad ones for the Bolshevik brand. An ill-advised attempt at a strategic alliance with Schickelgruber's, an aggressive new German franchise, ended in disaster. The names Leningrad and Stalingrad will forever be remembered from that period as examples of poor service and unusual burger ingredients. But Schickelgruber's was finally seen off and the Bolshevik brand entered a new phase of expansion. It was time, said Uncle Joe, to export Lenin's legacy to the world.

This wasn't an unqualified success. What goes down well in Kharkov can cause indigestion in Kabul. The expansion policy did net Bolshevik the important Chinese market, but even there, Russian attempts to include cabbage in Chinese burgers were soon met by Chinese demands that all Bolshevik meals include a side-order of rice. Before long, there were two competing Bolshevik brands, and then three once the Albanians got in on the act.

It was the beginning of the end. Weakened by the massive costs of enforcing brand compliance in territories as diverse as Kazakhstan and Cuba, the Bolshevik empire collapsed in debts and squabbling. It was all over for one of the major franchises of the twentieth century.

For a nostalgic reminder of those days, take a trip to the Finland Station, where you can still see a statue of Lenin addressing the workers, burger in one hand, fries in the other.

WIN A DAY WITH MIKHAIL GORBACHEV!

A Melodrama in Four Parts

I. Off to Work

Mikhail Gorbachev's day begins much like that of any busy western executive. After a vigorous session of sexual intercourse, Mikhail and his wife Raisa (a former student of philosophy at Moscow University who now drives a tractor in the Ukraine) enjoy a leisurely shower together before descending the central staircase of their modest Kremlin apartment to a hearty breakfast. Mikhail, trained as a lawyer, puts on the toast while Raisa brews up a stiff samovar of tea.

Over the breakfast table, Mick and Raisa chat about the news in the morning's *Pravda* and the hot gossip amongst their circle of friends — mostly the latest titillating details of Soviet Premier Nikolai Tikhonov's infatuation with a twenty-two-year-old Intourist guide — before sticking the dishes in the machine and heading off to work. For Raisa, it's now just a matter of setting the matter transmitter for the banks of the Dnieper and stepping through to the collective farm; for Mikhail, it's a brisk walk across the back yard to his regular job as General Secretary of the Central Committee of the Communist Party of the Soviet Union.

Wednesday the fifteenth of May is a comparatively light day for Mikhail, who arrives at the office at 9am sharp, exchanging quips about last night's dismal tour performance by Moscow Dynamo (they lost 1–5 to Punta Arenas FC) with his guards as he pushes open the swing doors of the Central Committee's open-plan office and heads for his desk at the back. After taking a quick look at the morning's intelligence bulletins — it appears Ronald Reagan has fallen off his horse again — he welcomes in the man ultimately responsible for preparing them, KGB Chief Viktor Chebrikov.

Viktor, who wears a terrible line in spectacles, is an affable, balding secret police professional. Today, he's looking more than usually pleased with himself, and the reason appears to be contained in a book he's carrying in his one good hand (the withering of the other is a legacy of the Sverdlovsk anthrax epidemic). The book, it transpires, is Arthur C. Clarke's *Expedition to Earth*.

II. Arthur C. Clarke

'Arthur C. Clarke,' notes Mikhail, a subscriber to the leading imperialist science fiction magazine *Analog*. 'Tell me, Viktor, how do you rate him in comparison with Asimov?'

'Well, as an SF writer, I think Clarke's got the edge. He brings a real quality of transcendence to his best work, so that it attains a numinous quality which belies his claim to be a writer of hard SF. *Expedition to Earth* showcases this well, I feel — stories like "Second Dawn", "Encounter in the Dawn", and, particularly, the title story have a haunting, evocative quality that derives in large part from the revelation of powerful contemporary motifs in unfamiliar and often ironic settings. "The Sentinel" is of course of special interest as the progenitor of *2001: A Space Odyssey* — have you seen the film, Mikhail?'

'I have. Almost as good as *Solaris*.'

'If you make allowances for its crypto-bourgeois philosophy,' Viktor said severely. 'And as for comparing Clarke with Asimov — Clarke's a fine writer, but I can't go past the fact that Asimov was born here.'

'True, Viktor, although I don't think we should let national chauvinism influence our literary judgements.'

'If you say so, boss. Anyway, getting back to *Expedition to Earth*, there's one story in it that appears particularly relevant in the light of Academician Ivanenko's recent investigations. Called "Loophole", it's cast in the epistolary form—'

'Letters, right?'

'Letters, yes. It starts with an exchange of missives between the ruler of Mars and his chief scientist. The Martians have just noticed the first atomic bomb test here on Earth, and — well, perhaps you'd like to read it for yourself, Mick?'

As Mikhail Gorbachev reads of the Martians' plans to dominate and eliminate the humans by controlling interplanetary space, and of the loophole through which the humans strike first, Viktor Chebrikov's gaze strays to the window at the other end of the room. On the other side of that window, the Lubyanka waits to receive its unwilling guests, three faceless bodies lie just beneath the melting snows of Gorky Park, and Arkady Renko sits with a small group of friends watching a smuggled videotape of *Hill Street Blues*.

In the snows east of Irkutsk, workers on the Baikal–Amur Mainline take care to prevent their skin from freezing to the track, and in the Tunguska the trees are again laid flat. Nude bathers are causing a stir in certain Black Sea resorts, whilst in a dacha just outside Moscow Nikolai Tikhonov gives his all in the arms of his beloved as KGB cameras record the scene for posterity.

And more coffins return through the mountain passes from Afghanistan, and Vladimir Arsenyev roams the taiga with his friend Dersu Uzala, and Stalin's daughter leaves and returns in pain, over and over, as the birches nod their heads in the breeze above the rich black Russian soil.

Mikhail Gorbachev finishes reading. 'Hmmm, matter

transmitters, eh? What a bright spark that Arthur C. Clarke is. Well, Viktor, any other news? Can my doctors be trusted?'

'Not a disloyal thought in their heads, Mick. I think you're safe there. But I must be going. I have an ethnic minority to oppress.'

'Which one?'

'Why, the Russians, of course!'

'One of these days we'll have to stop laughing at that joke. Well, Viktor, show that story to our good friend the Marshal. Our team at Tyuratam may be able to make something of it.'

'Okay, boss, I'm away. See you at the Politburo meeting.'

Mikhail spends the rest of the morning going through his paperwork and reading his mail; there are five circulars, two chain letters, one misdirected subscription to the satirical magazine *Krokodil* and no invitations to the Vatican. At lunchtime, there's time for a brisk game of squash with Vitaly Vorotnikov before the 2pm Politburo meeting.

III. The Politburo

The Politburo traditionally met in a sombre, marbled room, sitting six to a side along a massive table. Mikhail felt that this arrangement wasn't conducive to increased productivity and efficiency, so had done away with the heavy table and got everybody to sit in a circle on the ground, on cushions lovingly sewn in one of the more obscure Central Asian republics. The older Politburo members were not entirely happy about this arrangement, and still grumbled about it when they thought themselves unobserved. However, the younger men (for there were no female members of this most exclusive club) seemed to like the arrangement, and at the moment it was these men — Vorotnikov, Egor Ligachev, Nikolai Ryzhkov, Chebrikov, Eduard Shevardnadze, and Gorbachev himself — who called the shots.

Everyone is in their seats by 2pm sharp, and Mikhail opens the meeting by pinning a big sheet of paper to the wall and asking for agenda items. Ligachev, who has charge of the minutes of the previous meeting, reminds everyone that the Geneva summit and the forthcoming grain harvest are matters that weren't finalised at the last meeting. New agenda items include progress on the Baikal–Amur Mainline (BAM) rerouting, another increase in funds for technical intelligence, and the colour scheme for the Politburo's new ZIL limousines.

The meeting opens with a sharing session, wherein each member lets the others know how he's feeling, so private, personal problems won't fester unacknowledged beneath the surface of the meeting. Nikolai Tikhonov announces that he has never felt better; Chebrikov winks at Gorbachev. Andrei Gromyko, now slightly deaf, queries why anyone would want to feel butter. Shevardnadze, newly appointed Foreign Minister, reveals he's had an exciting day broadening his knowledge of geography, and now knows where Africa and Australia are. Someone whistles a derisory bar or two of 'Georgia on My Mind'. Generally, everyone is having a good day, although Vorotnikov claims Gorbachev has obstructed him on a couple of key points — then must hasten to explain he is talking about the lunchtime squash game rather than matters of state.

The Geneva summit (where Mikhail plans to try for a propaganda coup by challenging Reagan to see who can stay on a horse the longest), BAM, a twenty-five per cent increase in funds for purchase of western microcomputers and microengineers, and the grain harvest (about which there was general agreement that having one would be a Good Idea) are all sorted out quite simply. As everyone fears, the big clash between Gorbachev's new guard and the remaining old-timers comes over the ZILs' paintwork.

The matter had first surfaced under Gorbachev's predecessor Konstantin Chernenko, and in keeping with the dour Siberian's approach, the normal black colour scheme had been approved. However, Geidar Aliyev had felt even at the time that something more dynamic was called for, and subsequently proposed a trendy metallic red with racing stripes down the sides. A reliable source, who did not wish to be named, claimed that Aliyev had originally been planning to include mag wheels and furry dice in the package, but decided this might lessen Politburo members' dignity in the eyes of the proletariat.

After Aliyev has put his proposal, there is an uneasy silence in the room. When Gorbachev, who is facilitating the meeting, asks if there is any disagreement, President

Andrei Gromyko rises to his feet.

'For twenty-five years, I was the Foreign Minister of the Soviet Union. For all that time, Soviet representatives maintained the most punctilious dignity and reserve. The western imperialists seek to portray us as barbarians, but we have shown that we are the true standard-bearers of civilisation. Our sober black ZIL limousines have long been an important part of our image as serious, responsible world leaders. I could never agree to such a proposal.'

'Does that means you'd be prepared to block consensus on it, Andrei?'

'Yes, Mikhail, I would.'

'Well, does anyone want to try to change Andrei's mind?'

Ligachev, who has a reputation for over-enthusiasm, rises to his feet.

'Listen, Andrei, we're living in the eighties now, not the fifties. We're talking marketing, we're talking positioning, we're talking selling ourselves in the marketplace. Today's Politburo needs to project a positive, up-market image, inspiring confidence amongst our customers. Professor Lysenko over at the Soviet Institute of Psychodemographics tells me their latest survey indicates that more Great Russians in the sixteen to twenty-five cohort know that Wham! recently played China than are aware that the Central Committee recently approved the latest five-year plan. Our collective name-recognition factor, with the understandable exception of Comrade Gorbachev, is less than that of Elton John's percussionist. The citizens of Ust-Kut have recently petitioned to have the name of their main street changed from *Lenin* Prospekt to *Lennon* Prospekt! When this sort of thing is happening in Ust-Kut, need I say more?'

(The citizens of Ust-Kut, a small but bustling city in the progressive Lake Baikal region, knew nothing of this implied slur on their modernity, and continued about their business in happy ignorance.)

'Egor, interesting as all this is, I don't see why it means we have to have red ZILs with racing stripes down the sides.'

'Because they're new! They're modern! They're positive! They project the go-ahead image we need. Personally, I'd be prepared to compromise on the racing stripes, but after all, Comrade Gromyko, red is the colour of our Union's flag. Are you suggesting we should change that?'

Mikhail senses that tempers are rising. A good facilitator must be able to strike a balance between non-interference when a meeting is flowing smoothly, and appropriate intervention when things are going off the rails. Now is a time for the latter.

'It's obvious we have considerable disagreement on this issue, and I don't think we can reach a consensus at this meeting. What I suggest is that a few people who've got strong feelings on the issue get together and see if they can work out a compromise proposal, or a new and better one, to present to the next meeting. I won't join that group myself, but stepping outside my role as facilitator I'd like to suggest a dual fleet, one in black for the more ceremonial occasions and one in red, with or without stripes, for trips to the movies and so forth. Are there any volunteers for the working party?'

Aliyev, Ligachev, Vorotnikov and, after some prompting, Gromyko, agree to meet soon to come up with a solution that can be presented to the next Politburo meeting. The present meeting closes with an evaluation; everyone (even Gromyko) agrees it has gone well. Under Brezhnev and Chernenko, everyone would have headed off for a few vodkas at this point, but the fate of Grigory Romanov and other victims of Gorbachev's anti-alcoholism drive persuades them all to settle, in the interim, for tea, coffee, and Milo. After the last cup has been smashed in the fireplace, there's just enough time for Mikhail to pick up his duffle bag from the office before heading home to cook tea.

IV. Expedition to Earth

After the evening meal, Raisa and Mikhail would normally head out to the theatre or a movie, or invite a few friends round for a Pepsi. Tonight, however, they're off to Sheremetyevo Airport to greet the winner of the US–Soviet Friendship Society's 'Win a Day with Mikhail Gorbachev!' competition. This competition attracted over ten thousand entries, despite unfavourable comment in the US media, and represents a significant propaganda victory for the Soviet Union. Contestants were required to write an essay on the subject 'US–Soviet Relations: Where to from Here?', and as a tie-breaker had been asked to complete, in twenty-five words or fewer, the sentence 'I would like to visit the Soviet Union because . . .'

The winner's essay stands head and shoulders above its competition. If the tie-breaker had been required, his entry would undoubtedly have been disqualified, as his sentence contains twenty-six words. It reads, 'I would like to visit the Soviet Union because I have in my possession complete design drawings of the prototype Strategic Defence Initiative anti-missile laser system.'

The winner calls himself Jim Beam, and he arrives from Heathrow Airport by Aeroflot. He is met as he steps off the plane by senior officers of Soviet military intelligence, who relieve him of a folder of drawings he obligingly presents to them, and after submitting to a final search he is permitted to meet the Gorbachevs and the press. After exchanging pleasantries, the threesome return to the Kremlin for a private get-acquainted chat in Mikhail and Raisa's apartment. 'That means private,' Mikhail insists, shooing away the lurking Kremlin guards.

When the door has closed behind the last of the guards, it is Raisa who speaks. 'We have been awaiting this meeting for a long time, Anatar. But why did you choose such a public method of arrival?'

The Ambassador to Earth of the Galactic Federation peels off the false head, legs and genitals, places them in a small attaché case, and squats before them in its true form. 'An old Earth custom, I believe — of hiding in plain sight. How could anyone so public as Mr Jim Beam be other than what he seemed? Well, we can dispense with Mr Beam now. How soon can you leave?'

'I've told my colleagues on the collective farm that I'm taking a week's holiday — I believe that will be sufficient? I've packed my bags, and we recovered the atmosphere suit and other equipment from the Tunguska a week ago. The matter transmitter brought them in easily. I'm ready when you are, Anatar,' responds Raisa.

'Very well. Mr Gorbachev, would you like to come with us to farewell your wife?'

'I certainly would. But there's one thing I don't understand, Anatar: why can't the matter transmitter take Raisa all the way to Galactic HQ?'

'I don't know, General Secretary. I'm a diplomat, not a scientist. But I've been told that both loci of the matter transmitter need to be on the same planetary body — something to do with frames of reference, I understand.'

'Science is a wonderful thing. I must introduce you to some of our more far-sighted writers on the subject.'

'Save the books for later, Mick,' says Raisa. 'It's time to go.'

The aliens' ship is waiting in a forest between Shar'ya and Kirov; their matter transmitter, of which an embarrassed Academician Ivanenko is still trying to provide a convincing explanation to the military, sends them through from Moscow one at a time. The ship is the conventional saucer shape. A ramp extends to the ground, and between the pine trees small figures on trolleys are moving through the mist, collecting specimens.

Before Raisa puts on her atmosphere suit and goes off to the headquarters of the Galactic Federation to present the case for Earth's admission, she and Mikhail say goodbye. They stand at the foot of the ramp, holding each other close.

'Keep everything ticking over while I'm away, won't you, Mick?'

'I don't expect any major problems. I'm sure we'll reach a compromise on the ZILs without Andrei losing face. Nothing else should be too difficult — for me. You're the one who's got the hard work ahead.'

'Oh, I think I'll manage okay. It's a formality, really, isn't it? Well, Anatar is looking impatient, probably. I have to go. I love you, darling. Take care.'

'I will. You take care too. I'll take a day off when you get back, eh?'

They hold hands as long as they can while Raisa seals herself into the suit. Then they separate, and she walks slowly up the ramp as the returning alien scientists whir past her. When they have all entered, the ramp is closed and the spaceship silently rises. As Mikhail turns to journey back to Moscow, the sky fills with light and a peal of thunder echoes over the sleeping land.

THE NEW NEIGHBOURS

High property values are the hallmark of a civilised society. Though our generation may never build cathedrals nor find a cure for cancer, may never save the whales nor end world hunger, yet we can die with smiles on our faces if we have left our homes better than we found them, if we have added decks, remodelled kitchens, and created indoor-outdoor flow.

Reaction in my street to the news that an alien family would soon move into number 56 was therefore mixed. Number 56 was the proverbial worst house on the best street, and any family who could improve it — regardless of skin colour or number of limbs — was welcome, in my view. My wife Alison said she'd wait and see. Josh wondered if they had any kids his age.

Others near to the action, and particularly the Murrays at 54 and the Zhangs at 58, were less sanguine. 'But it's not as if they need a resource consent,' said my wife to Jessica Zhang, and she was right. Having bought the house at a legitimate auction through a telephone bidder, and paid the deposit, the alien family were well within their rights to settle in our street, and the rest of us would simply have to make the best of it.

To the unpractised eye, the twelfth of March would have seemed little different from any other late summer Saturday in Utley Terrace. Eight o'clock was the usual bleary-eyed rush-hour of parents taking their children to cricket. By half past eleven, when Josh and I returned to our place at number 55, there was a little more activity: a lawn being mowed, a car being washed, the postie delivering bills and special offers. All the same, a certain twitching at curtains spoke of suppressed excitement.

Hoping for a flying saucer, we were disappointed when a perfectly ordinary moving van appeared outside number 56 shortly after noon, and perfectly ordinary movers began carrying an assemblage of furniture — not well colour-coordinated, but not notably alien — into the house. Half an hour later, a white Toyota Corolla pulled up outside, and our new neighbours, who went by the name of Thompson, got out. We stood at our lounge room window, staring.

They looked completely human: Mum, Dad and the three kids. One appeared to be a teenager, I was perturbed to note — did alien teenagers play Marilyn Manson loud at 3am? Dressed in practical moving-day clothes, they looked right at home as they took possession of their new domain.

'That's pretty boring,' said Josh. 'They look just like us.'

'There's a reason for that,' said Alison. 'They're shape-shifters.'

'Cool!' said Josh. 'How many different shapes do you reckon they can turn into?'

'As many as they like, but they can't change their mass,' Alison told him. She had this on good authority from her friend Cecile in Wellington. Cecile, said Alison, had contacts.

We didn't usually do anything special to welcome new people to the street, but in this case, we thought we should make an exception. Neither the Murrays not the Zhangs could be expected to take the lead. The Murrays, acting on the adage that good fences make good neighbours, had already added a metre to the height of theirs. Alison and I decided it was up to us. We rang round, got a dozen or so pledges of support, and then went over the road to knock on the new neighbours' door.

It was opened by the teenager, who looked us up and down, called over her shoulder something that must have meant 'Mum!', and disappeared back inside without another word. So far, so human.

Mum came to the door. There was something unusual about her face. I don't mean that she had three eyes, or purple skin, or a ring of small feeding tentacles where her mouth should have been. Her features were quite regular and normal, but they lacked any distinguishing quirks. Her nose, her eyes, her ears, her mouth: all were in proportion, and her skin was flawless, without a beauty spot or wrinkle to break the monotony. She looked like everyone and no one.

'Good evening. How may I help you?' she said.

'We were — some of your neighbours were . . .' I stumbled to embarrassed silence, and Alison took over.

'Your new neighbours would like to meet you and your family,' said Alison, 'and we thought, perhaps, we could host a little celebration to welcome you to our street. We thought we'd pop over first, say hello, and ask when might be a good time.'

'Excuse me, please,' said the woman, and returned inside.

We waited on the doorstep, straining our ears for noises within. Something that might have been music drifted from the back of the house.

'I bet they're consulting with their superiors,' said Josh. 'I bet they have an antenna in the back yard.'

There were three Super 14 games on that evening, and I had twenty bucks on the Blues by twelve or under. My feet were making small movements back from the doorstep when the woman reappeared.

'Now is a good time,' she said. 'And we will host the occasion.'

'Now?'

'We possess and have studied a barbecue.'

It was short notice, and there was some grumbling among the invited guests at this breach of protocol, but curiosity won out, and a pretty good crowd soon gathered in the Thompsons' back yard. Even Jessica Zhang popped over for five minutes before excusing herself. While I helped George to fire up the barbie, Alison inducted Myrtle into the mysteries of impromptu salads, and once a few of the lads turned up with some Speight's, the party was humming.

'Do you, er, do you — make sure you keep turning them, they burn easy — do you eat our sort of food, then?'

'When we look as you do, we eat as you do,' George said.

'It's true, then, you can change your shape?'

'We change to suit our environment.'

I took another swig of Speight's. 'What do you really look like?'

For a moment, something green and as broad as tall stood before me, balanced on an indeterminate number of legs. Bony plates clashed in its jaw.

'Watch out, mate,' I said as he returned to human form, 'you've dropped the tongs.'

Later that night, when George and Myrtle had put Lucy and Peter to bed, and shouted goodnight to the teenaged Susan through her locked door, I sat in a deck-chair in number 56's back yard, with Josh a heavy, sleepy weight against my legs. George sat beside me. The girls were inside somewhere, looking at paint samples.

'Where are you from?' I asked.

'In your terms, it's Carina -59°23',' said George. He pointed, and I looked. Nothing but a faint wisp of stars.

'Must be a long way,' I said.

'It is.'

'No popping back home for a holiday, then.'

'Not in a hurry, no.'

'So why'd you come here, George?'

'To build a better future for our children,' said George.

You couldn't argue with that.

The trouble started at school. We were proud of Rosemont Primary's decile 10 rating, and guarded it jealously. There may have been more government money to be had by dropping down a decile or two, but the effect on morale would have been disastrous.

So Rosemont Primary strove for excellence in all things. That caused problems when it came to school sports day. Josh was bursting to tell me about it when I picked him up from after-school care.

'Lucy from over the road won the 100 metres, and Karen Pihama got mad at her and said she cheated and grew some extra legs in the middle of the race, and Karen said aliens ought to go back where they came from, and Mrs Grenville told her off, and then Lucy said she did grow some extra legs, but she didn't know she wasn't supposed to. And Lucy made the team for the Northern Zone finals and Karen didn't. And Karen says her mummy will sue the school.'

In the end, the school sent both of them to the finals, and made Lucy promise to stick to a human body shape.

Legal action was averted, but it was a straw in the wind.
Off work one day with a cold, I went to pick up Josh at
3pm. There was a tight knot of mothers standing to one
side of the netball goal, and Myrtle Thompson standing
on the other side by herself.

I sidled close to the group.

'. . . disgusting, they have every advantage, and the
school doesn't . . .'

'. . . won't put up with . . .'

'. . . start a petition?'

I left the mothers to their anger, and went over to
Myrtle. Perhaps she was adapting to our world: faint lines
of worry had appeared around her eyes.

'Tough day?'

She ghosted a smile. 'Lucy came first in another test.
The other children say it isn't fair, and now their mothers
are getting upset. I tell her not to stand out so much, to
come second sometimes, but it's not in her nature.'

'How about Peter?'

'He's turning into a real Kiwi boy. Ignores his
schoolwork, spends all his time on his PlayStation or
kicking a rugby ball around. He's fitting in fine.'

Then the bell rang, and Josh — not quite old enough
yet to be embarrassed by his father — came bounding out
of the classroom to bury me beneath a blizzard of school
notices.

The Concerned Parents' meeting was supposed to be
by invitation only, and as known allies of the aliens, we
weren't in the loop. But nothing stays secret for long in

Utley Terrace, and the Thompsons found out even before we did. We made some calls, and got together with the Thompsons for a strategy session.

'But what can the Concerned Parents actually do?' I asked.

'Their first step is to get our children suspended, or preferably expelled, from school. If they can do that, they deduce that we'll move away. From what I've heard, Karen Pihama's mother will move to challenge our immigration status if that doesn't work out.'

'I told Lucy she should have chosen someone other than a lawyer's daughter to beat in that race,' George added unhelpfully.

'What are they going to get your children suspended for? Both of them are good kids and a credit to the school. And you've paid your fees.'

'Some of the other kids are starting to gang up on them, on Lucy especially. They're trying to provoke a reaction. Lucy's doing her best, but it's hard for her. Perhaps we should do what they want?'

'It's the problem with being pioneers,' said George. 'Wherever we go, we will face these attitudes. I think we should stay here and face these critics down. I think we should attend the meeting of the Concerned Parents' Group.'

Meeting Room 4 at the Rosemont Community Centre, 7.22pm. The Concerned Parent at the door looked up in alarm as George, Myrtle, and Susan arrived, flanked by their supporters.

'You can't come in here,' hissed the Concerned Parent, who happened to be Leonie Murray from number 54.

'Why not?'

'This is a private meeting.'

'No it's not,' I said. 'It's a public meeting, because you're meeting in a community centre paid for by everyone's rates. We have just as much right to be here as you have.' We swept past her into the room.

Much consternation, much gathering and whispering among the organisers. Eventually, Leonie Murray walked up to the lectern with a smile pasted to her face.

'Good evening, everyone. Tina kowtow, tina kowtow, tina kowtow car-tower.' I saw Huhana Pihama wince at the multiple mispronunciations. 'We all know why we're here,' Leonie said, and glared at us, the tight knot of Thompsons and supporters in the third and fourth rows back. 'We've built up a cohesive little community here in Utley Terrace, a community that shares certain values, and now that community is threatened. The government won't do anything, and the City Council won't do anything, and the school says it can't do anything, so it's time we did something ourselves. It seems that news of this meeting spread a bit wider than we planned, so we're going to adjourn the meeting here and reconvene at 54 Utley Terrace, where only those who've got a genuine commitment to this community are invited to attend.'

Myrtle Thompson rose to her feet. 'Before you go off to your little meeting, I want to say something,' she said, to cries of 'Sit down!' and 'Go back where you came from!' She did not sit down. One or two of the staunchest Concerned Parents walked from the room, but the rest of the audience stayed, waiting for something to happen.

It did. Myrtle changed shape, and once again, but for longer this time, I saw one of our new neighbours in its true form. There was nothing too threatening there: no claws, no tentacles, no teeth to speak of. A multi-limbed green blob, with a mouth pleading for air: Myrtle was breathing heavily by the time she changed back to human form. Three more people had scrambled out of their seats and left in a hurry, but Myrtle had the rest of the audience hooked.

'This is who I am,' she said when she got her breath back. 'I am not the same as you, but I do not threaten you. For millennia, we of Th'katath have spread throughout the galaxy, seeking only to live peaceably with our neighbours, to trade with them, to invest in their worlds.

'You are a nation of traders. You send your sheep, your beef, your wool, your fruit across to the other side of your planet. But do you not realise what riches are on offer to those who trade among the stars? Look!'

Without any visible means of projection, she made glowing images appear on the off-white wall of Meeting Room 4, and she began her pitch. She told us that we in New Zealand, little old New Zealand, had what the galaxy was craving: fresh air, solitude, and the leanest lamb in the galaxy. Tourists, she promised, would flock to see us; carbon-based life forms everywhere, those of a carnivorous persuasion, wouldn't be able to get enough of our two-tooth and hogget.

'Why don't you tell the government?' asked Larry Purvis from the quantity surveyor's.

'We have. But we will not trade with those who hate us, and so we came to live among you, to see whether we would be welcomed or shunned. Perhaps we should have known that we would find a little of each reaction. Now is your time to decide. Will you have us, and the riches we bring?'

High property values are the hallmark of a civilised society. Meeting Room 4 said yes. Overwhelmingly, they said yes. They came up and apologised; they offered handshakes and hugs; they asked whether the inhabitants of the galaxy might find a use for batik, or management consulting, or quantity surveyors. They left happier than they arrived, and even those who were parents were, for the most part, concerned no longer.

Of course, not everyone was happy. Lucy and Peter still had to put up with the odd comment in the playground, and there were still some who edged away whenever one of the Thompsons came into a room. Number 54 Utley Terrace squatted behind its high fence and its locked gate, and would have no part of the bright future on offer. But otherwise the mood was all for change.

And change duly came. Myrtle and George don't live at number 56 any more — they've gone back to the home world. Lucy and Peter, and Peter's PlayStation, went with them, but Susan stayed on in the house. She met a nice human boy from Palmerston North, and they've got a family of their own now, two girls and a boy on the way. The children look human enough, and beyond that, I'm too much the gentleman to ask.

Myrtle wasn't lying about the rest of the galaxy. Energy is as cheap as chips up there, and galactics — those who can breathe our air — come in such numbers the government's had to put restrictions on the back country. Lots of Chinese and Indian restaurants are closing down and being replaced by New Zealand ones, and you can walk past any bistro and see aliens of all shapes and sizes dining out on puha, kumara, and lamb.

There's just Alison and me now. Josh studied engineering in Christchurch, then, a couple of years ago, he left on a longer journey. We drove him up to Shannon, then stood watching from a safe distance, behind 80 centimetres of reinforced glass, as the spear of light rose straight up into the night sky. Neither of us had much to say on the drive home.

Tonight we're out on the deck, using the telescope that Myrtle and George gave us as a parting gift. Golden lights move serenely through the field of view, far above Earth's atmosphere. We swing our telescope towards the patch of sky, dark and almost empty, where we know our son now lives, studying, learning. Sometimes we get a message: Josh smiling and telling us he's fine against a background of lights, or of bodies with too many legs, or places we cannot recognise or even comprehend.

I'm retired, and Alison isn't far off. One day soon, we'll sell our house — the worst house on the best street — and after a few weeks of touring around and saying goodbye to friends, we'll take that road to Shannon. Before they left, George and Myrtle said to look them up one day. I think we will.

SISTERS

Sisters under the skin, Kapiti and Mana guarded the coastal waters.

Kapiti was beautiful. When she tossed her green-crowned head, flocks of birds rose up in her honour. She was queen of the coast.

To the south, Mana waited for better days. The grass which had long been her only coat hissed in the wind. She gazed at Kapiti in love and envy.

One night, when envy waxed stronger, Mana cast off from her moorings, extended her kelp-covered limbs, and set off to visit ruin upon her sister. In those days, Mana was covered in sheep. Near the woolshed, shepherds had made fire for their comfort. Mana knew where the embers smouldered, knew that one spark cast aloft could reduce her sister's crowning glory to ashes. As the northerly howled, Mana moved to the windward side of Kapiti.

She was almost in position when Kapiti awoke and saw her. 'It is a long time since we lay this close together, sister,' said Kapiti.

Mana did not reply.

'Have you come to marvel at my trees, my birds, the waves that break to foam against my sides?'

Mana continued to move northward. She must strike once, and quickly.

'I see that something troubles you. The sheep have shorn you. Come to my lee side, and my trees will waft seed to you on the breeze. Nurture this gift, and in time your coat will rival mine.'

Mana halted, rolling in the swell. Her sister was arrogant, but Mana had never known her to lie. Changing course, Mana moved to leeward. The wind blew drifts of seed to settle on her grass.

'There,' said Kapiti. 'You may leave me now.'

Mana was back in her accustomed place by dawn. As the days passed, the precious seed was consumed by sheep, washed out to sea, blown onto barren stone. The gift had been squandered, and Mana resigned herself to misery.

Times changed. The sheep were removed, and the grass grew longer. Mice plagued Mana, but the plague passed. Boats came from the mainland with seedlings. Planted with care, they thrived and grew. Now, on bitter nights, Mana does not feel the wind so keenly.

'Kapiti,' she calls one night, 'look at me now! Soon I will be as beautiful as you!'

There is no reply, for Kapiti is sleeping. But in her

dreams, two sisters, heavy with bird and flower, sail down the years together.

NOT WANTED ON VOYAGE

Emma and Mummy went for a walk along the beach. Mummy carried the picnic hamper. Emma ran in front of her, chasing Davy and looking at the waves.

Emma watched the waves racing across the sand. They raced and raced, and then they got slower and stopped. Sometimes they stopped right beside her feet, or even washed over them. Then they ran back down the beach and into the sea. Emma wanted to chase after them, but Mummy said she couldn't. Emma said she had her gumboots on, and she wouldn't get her feet wet. Mummy said yes she would, and not to be a naughty girl.

Mummy let Davy go in the sea, and sometimes she threw sticks way out into the water for him to chase. Davy ran into the waves and started to swim after them. Usually he found them and carried them back in his mouth, but once he couldn't find the stick Mummy had thrown. He swam around in circles and then he started swimming away into the sea. Mummy called 'Davy!' very loud. She was scared that he might swim away for ever and not come back. Emma was scared, too, and she called as well. Davy came back after a while and ran to Mummy. She told him off and said she was never going to throw him a stick again. Davy shook himself and got Mummy all wet.

Mummy said it was time for a rest. She sat down on a log and had a smoke. Emma sat near her and looked for the moon. She loved the moon. She was too little to stay up all night and watch it, but sometimes you could see it in the day. She looked and looked, and then she saw it. It was hard to see.

There were some birds, and Davy chased them. He almost caught one, but then it flew away. The birds were black and white, and had funny red legs. They walked along the sand until Davy got very near to them, then they flew away. They made a funny noise, too. It made Emma feel lonely. She was happy when she and Mummy started walking again.

It took a long time to get to the picnic place. Emma got very tired, and she could hardly walk. Even Davy was just trotting along beside them with his tongue hanging out. 'I'm sorry, dear,' said Mummy, 'I had no idea it was this far. Isn't everything such a long way in this country?' Emma didn't know what a country was.

Where they stopped to eat, there were some tables with little seats along the side of them — picnic tables, Mummy called them. There were some swings and a slide, too.

They didn't use the picnic tables, because Mummy had brought a blanket that she laid on the ground. It was red and white. There were sandwiches, and cakes, and Mummy had some coffee in a flask.

'That's Daddy's flask,' said Emma. She remembered him carrying it one time.

'That's right, dear,' said Mummy. 'I've got some fizz for you.' It was in a brown bottle.

Emma said she wanted to do wees, and Mummy took her behind some bushes. If this was a proper picnic ground, Mummy said, there would be some toilets. Everything in this country is so primitive, she said. Emma said she would like to have a play now.

After Emma had played on the swings and the slide, she helped put away the picnic things. Mummy had another smoke, then they started walking back down the beach. By the time they got back to their house, it was getting dark. The moon was a lot brighter, and the sun had gone away. 'Look, Mummy,' said Emma, 'the sun has gone in a hole.' Mummy smiled and told her she was a good girl.

The next day Emma went to kindergarten. She didn't like it very much, and she often told Mummy that she wanted to stay home and help her instead, but Mummy said she had to go, because it was good for her to play with other children. Emma didn't think it was good at all, because she didn't like those children. They were silly and nasty, and they called her names. They weren't her friends. She had lots of friends where they used to live. Now just Davy and her doll Judy and Teddy were her friends. Mummy was her friend, too, but Mummy was a bit grumpy sometimes.

At the kindergarten, there was a teacher called Mrs Scott. Mrs Scott was quite nice, and if Emma was upset she gave her a cuddle, but then she said she had to go away and play again. Emma liked to play with the dolls and the tea set. She liked to play with the cars, too.

She had some cars at home, and sometimes Mummy bought her a new car. When she got a new car, she would take it to visit all the other cars. The new car would say 'Hello' to each of her old cars. The old car would ask, 'What's your name?', then the new car would say its name, and they would have a talk.

When all the cars had said hello to the new car, Emma would line the cars up on the living room floor and drive them across to the kitchen. Sometimes they got stuck in the mud, and the big bulldozer had to push them out. The big bulldozer was a present from Daddy. There were big bulldozers like that where he was working. She wanted to go and live with Daddy and drive bulldozers and graders and make roads, like Daddy did. Mummy could come and live there, too.

There were lots of cars at the kindergarten. Whenever Emma started playing with the cars at the kindergarten, boys grabbed them off her. One day, when she had got all the cars at the kindergarten lined up, a boy kicked them all away and hit her. Then she hit him back. When Emma told on the boy, Mrs Scott said, 'Well, dear, the cars are mainly for the boys to play with. Why don't you come and play with the tea set? You like that, don't you?' So Emma went and played with the tea set.

Today they had painting. They put on special aprons, and Mrs Scott gave them big sheets of brown paper and the different paints, and a brush each, and water to wash it in. Emma heard Mrs Scott tell one of the other ladies that she didn't enjoy painting much, because everything got so messy, but that it was important for the children to express themselves.

Emma was good at painting. She painted trees, and flowers, and bulldozers, and the house they used to live in before they went on the big ship. She tried to paint Davy, too, but he came out looking all funny.

Her mummy came to take her home. Mrs Scott said, 'Can I have a word with you, Mrs Walters?' Mummy and Mrs Scott talked for a long time, and then they looked at Emma's pictures. Mummy looked worried. She said, 'Emma, darling, why are your pictures always so black? The houses are black, the trees are black, even the people are black.'

'There's some red there,' said Emma. 'That's a flower.'

'They're very nice pictures, dear,' said Mummy. She looked at her watch and said it was time to catch the bus.

'Don't worry too much, Mrs Walters,' said Mrs Scott. 'It's bound to take her time to adjust. You know, I've got friends from Home who—'

'Yes, I'm sure we'll be quite all right, thank you,' said Mummy, and they went to catch the bus. Mummy let Emma pull the cord when it was time to get off. When they arrived home, Emma went to see Davy, who was tied up in his kennel. He was very pleased to see her.

The next day, Emma was playing in the front garden when she saw the postman. He said 'Hello' to her. Davy barked at him, but Emma said 'Hello' back. 'There's some mail for you and your mummy,' said the postman. 'Do you want to take it to her?' Emma said she did. There were two letters. They both had stamps with a picture of a lady's head.

'That's a bill,' said Mummy, putting the first letter to one side, 'but this one's a letter from Daddy!'

'I want to read it,' said Emma.

'You come and sit up here next to me, and we'll both read it.' So they sat on the sofa and read Daddy's letter. Emma didn't know how to read, so she looked at the words on the page and thought about Daddy.

'Well, dear, Daddy's written a special letter just for you. This is what it says. "Dear Emma" — there's the letter E for Emma — "I hope you are well, and that you are enjoying life by the sea. Mummy tells me that you are going to kindergarten. Have you made friends with any of the other children? I wish you and Mummy could come and live with me, but Mr Jackson, who is in charge of the construction work here, says that the house for us all to live in won't be ready for another six months. That's a long time to wait, but in two more months I will be coming home for Christmas to see you. Please be a good girl and do what Mummy says. Love, Daddy."'

Then Emma cried because she missed Daddy. When

she had stopped crying, Mummy said, 'Daddy's written an extra bit, called a PS. It says "I was talking today with Mr O'Rourke, who drives the big grader, and he promised that he would give you a ride on it when you and Mummy come to live here. That's something to look forward to! Love, Dad."'

Emma was very excited about having a ride on the grader. She asked if she would have to have a big sleep before she could ride on it, and Mummy said, 'I'm afraid so, dear. Quite a few big sleeps.' So Emma asked Mummy to get her toy grader and bulldozer, the ones Daddy had bought for her, and she went out to the sandpit and played for hours and hours. The sandpit was near the back fence, and when the grader and the bulldozer were tired from pushing lots of sand and needed to have a sleep, Emma went to the back fence and looked out between the boards at the sea. A big ship was sailing there. Emma rushed inside and woke Mummy, who was having a nap.

'Mummy! I saw our ship!'

Mummy had a look over the fence, and then Mummy and Emma quickly put on their coats and went down to the beach. A stiff northerly was blowing, and the wind whipped up the waves and sent the sand hissing along the beach, so that Mummy picked up Emma and held her close. A white ship was sailing out of the harbour, a large white ship with 'P&O' on the funnel. 'It's not a ferry, is it, Mummy? It's our ship, that we came on!'

'Our ship, going Home,' agreed Mummy. Mummy talked about 'Home' a lot. She looked sad when she talked about it. Emma thought Home was the place she used to live with Mummy and Daddy, before they came here. Emma liked it at Home. She had friends there who were other children. Mummy used to have the other mummies over for tea. They would laugh and talk a lot. Home had a horse that lived in the field behind their house, and a big building down the lane with blades that went round and round in the wind. Mummy told her that was where the miller lived.

Emma slipped from Mummy's grasp and ran along the shore. If she could catch the ship, she could go home and be with all her friends, and play in the garden with the apple trees and the swing.

The big ship was going fast along the channel on the outward tide. Emma ran into the waves. The water was deep and cold, and suddenly a wave came and swept over the top of her gumboots. Emma stumbled backwards and sat down, and just then Mummy picked her up, and smacked her bottom, and asked her what in goodness' name she was doing, and didn't she know she could have drowned? But Emma just said, 'I want to go on the ship, Mummy. I want to go Home!' She started to shiver.

'Oh, you're wet through!' said Mummy. She wrapped Emma in her big coat and carried her back to their rented wooden bungalow, with the blue paint peeling in the salt-laden wind, and the stillborn flowers in the garden, and the crates full of their former lives, still sealed with metal strips, standing in Emma's bedroom with 'Not Wanted on Voyage' stencilled across them in large, black letters.

JIM CLARK

When we get up, it's hosing down, so we take the car. If race day is sunny, we usually walk, though it's a long way for my eight-year-old legs. Today the rain stops as the line of traffic crawls its way towards Teretonga, and the Southland summer sun tries to find a way through.

Our red Mini pulls into the car park at Sandy Point Domain. White-coated marshals from the Southland Car Club direct the car along narrow tracks through the marram grass and collect the parking fee. Finally the car comes to a halt at the end of a row of other cars. Dad takes up his haversack, which contains our raincoats and the food Mum has packed for us. We set off under the pines and between the dunes.

The sound that draws us onwards is the sound of excitement, that note somewhere between a sewing machine and a hornet, magnified a thousand-fold, painful and beautiful, that waxes and wanes as each car approaches and recedes. 'Hurry up,' I say to Dad, 'or we'll miss the race!' We keep going until, from the top of a low sandhill, we can see the last two laps of the current race. It's the Mini 7s, at the sewing machine end of the sonic spectrum, their drivers flinging the brave little machines along the back straight and into the sweeping right-hander. They race around the corner and out of our sight. On the main straight, someone is bringing out a chequered flag. A final crescendo from that direction, drifting towards us on the wind, then the engines fall silent.

There are a thousand places to sit and stand. Amid the low dunes and the lupins, families have staked out their vantage points on the dry, sandy soil. Local haulage firms have turned the backs of sheep trucks into grandstands for the day. We are heading for the main grandstand, a lengthy assemblage of planks and scaffolding on the north side of the main straight.

It's a long walk down the back straight, round the hairpin, and along half of the main straight to the grandstand, where marshals stand ready to exact a further toll. As we walk, the silence is broken by another roar of engines, throatier than the previous batch, deeper: the Big Bangers, Australian and American V8s, have come out to play. They accelerate like stampeding rhinos and turn like pigs, and the point of the hairpin is the perfect place to view their almost comical inability to take corners. I want to stand there for the rest of the race, but Dad hasn't forgotten that two kids around my age were killed at

Teretonga two years ago when a car went off the track and smashed into them. He hurries me away to somewhere a little higher and a lot safer.

'I wish the V8s were racing the Minis today,' I say when we've got to the end of the home straight. Dad agrees. We like nothing better than to see the Minis dart past the V8s under braking and hold them off through the curves along the back of the course, though everyone knows that the V8s will roar to the front again along the home straight, leaving the Minis in their wake on the final run to the flag.

Six laps of thunder, and a two-abreast race towards the chequered flag; someone has won and someone has lost, but there's no telling who from this distance. It doesn't matter, anyway. We're here for the big race, the 1968 Teretonga International, Round 4 of the Tasman Series. Every year the world's top Formula One drivers — men like Jackie Stewart, Piers Courage, and New Zealand's own Bruce McLaren, Denny Hulme and Chris Amon — come down under for eight weeks of racing: four weeks in New Zealand and four more in Australia. In 2.5 litre cars, they spend summer racing around the narrow, bumpy circuits of Australasia, with the local racers in smaller, older cars trailing along behind them. All the Formula One heroes whose exploits we devour each month in *Motor Sport* magazine walk among us for a few hours — or, at least, they walk around the pits and the infield. And then their cars are rolled out to the grid, four abreast on the narrow track, and they get down to work.

It will be the best part of an hour before the big

race starts. We climb up the widely spaced planks of the grandstand and take our seats halfway up, about a hundred yards down the track from the start-finish line. From here, we will be able to see the cars accelerating along the main straight, braking for the hairpin, and then making their way along the short back straight and into the Esses, where we'll lose sight of them among the dunes.

The sun ducks and dives between the clouds. The wind is still chilly, and I sit next to Dad, huddled in my raincoat, while he takes the lunchbox and the Thermos out of the haversack. On race days, I get to drink coffee from the Thermos. We eat filled rolls and fruit cake. There's orange juice as well.

Neither Mum nor my sister wanted to go to the racing. We'll be happy at home, they said. You go and enjoy yourselves.

It's never happened before, and I don't know why it happens now. Maybe, tummy full and mind at ease, I fall asleep for a moment. The next thing I know, I'm lying on the ground, looking up at a tangled view that resolves itself into wooden planks, metal scaffolding, and the anxious faces of my father and two adults I don't know. Bits of me are sore.

'Ask him something,' says a woman.

'How many fingers am I holding up?' asks Dad.

'Two,' I reply. I start to sit up, but the woman shakes her head.

'Where are we?' Dad asks, pushing me gently back down.

'At Teretonga, of course! We're not missing the race, are we?' Then I realise that's a silly question. There are no motors revving, no one's changing through the gears.

'I'm not hurt,' I say. 'What happened?'

'I don't know,' says Dad. 'There was a shout and a thump. When I turned round, I couldn't see you. This lady said you'd fallen between the planks.'

'Out like a light, you were,' says the lady. The man beside her, his face red below a trilby hat, nods solemnly.

'How do you feel?' asks Dad.

'All right, but I think I scraped my side.'

There is some grazing and a long, shallow cut. Dad reaches up for the haversack, gets out the first aid kit, and treats me with Savlon and plasters. 'What do you think?' he asks.

'I'm fine,' I say. 'How do we get back up?'

'You need to watch out,' says the lady, 'these things don't always show up right away. Watch for a straw-coloured fluid coming out of his nose, persistent headaches, unexplained memory loss, that sort of thing.'

'Do you have a headache?' asks the man in the trilby hat.

'No, thanks,' I reply.

I can see from Dad's expression that he has received all the help and advice from strangers that he can tolerate, but that he doesn't wish to be rude. 'I'll be fine,' I assure the watching couple. 'I think the race must be starting soon.'

Dad escorts me out to the edge of the grandstand,

then we clamber back to our seats. Dad tells me I still have a head for heights.

The lady and the man with the hat take their places to our right. The lady smiles at me as she sits down. I smile back.

No sooner have we sat down than another skiff of rain comes over, wetting us, wetting the track. I sit there feeling damp, cold and miserable. I think of Mum and my sister, safe and warm at home. I feel like crying. Then the sun comes out, leading the Tasman Series cars onto the grid.

Our hero isn't some showy European or exotic South American. Our hero is Jim Clark, a farmer's son from Fifeshire. He made his name in rallies and hill climbs in Scotland before switching to single seaters and becoming the best Formula One driver of his generation. I can imagine being Jim Clark, a modest man with a special gift for driving fast. Of course, everyone out there has that gift, even the slowest back-marker trundling around the course in a second-hand Brabham, but Jim Clark is faster than anyone else.

There is nothing like the sound of twenty-one single-seater racing cars firing up on the grid, then accelerating, as slowly at first as a Saturn V rocket leaving the launchpad, down the main straight. They race past the grandstand and along to the hairpin, where, as close as possible to the corner, they decelerate again, downshifting through the gears. By the time they get there, Jim Clark is already in the lead, his Lotus 49T — sleeker, fitter, faster — a low-slung blur down the back straight and into the esses. The rest of the cars straggle out behind him, and the scream of engines recedes into the distance as they negotiate the far side.

With the race safely underway, we settle down for the long haul. Sixty laps to go. Each lap, we peer at the cars as they come into view, trying to see whether Amon has passed Rodriguez, or whether there is an unexpected gap in the running order which means that someone has come a cropper around the back of the circuit. We yell deduction and speculation at each other over the roar of the engines. There's always something to see, and if there isn't, there's certainly something to hear.

It comes on to rain again, blowing into our faces, turning the track into a skating rink.

Jim Clark looks like he has this race sewn up. He should slow down a little, take no chances, and cruise to victory. But that's not him. As I hear the man in the trilby hat say to his wife, he's going full tit. I didn't know men said that sort of thing to their wives.

It happens on lap 53, just past the start-finish line. Jim Clark is accelerating along the main straight when his car hits a bump and flies into the air. I can see it so clearly, right in front of me. Jim Clark is flying. If the car flips over and lands on top of him, he'll die. If it lands on its wheels, he should be fine. Fear pins me to my seat. I don't pray. I don't cry out. If he—

The car slews around in flight and veers off towards the infield, but it stays upright. It lands on its wheels. It bounces backwards and stops. We crane our necks. Then the car is moving again. He's driving it into the pits! My weightless stomach drops back into place.

Bruce McLaren is in the lead now, but that doesn't really matter, because Jim Clark is alive and well. Well enough, in fact, to rejoin the race from the pits and set off after the leaders; well enough, though his car is missing its nose cone, for him to push Bruce McLaren all the way to the chequered flag. McLaren wins, but he's just a driver. Jim Clark is a hero, a man without fear. I'm almost too tired to eat dinner, but I'm still talking about the race as they cart me off to bed.

Seventy-one days later, Jim Clark is dead. My father tells me the news at breakfast. He was taking part in some meaningless Formula Two race at the Hockenheimring — Formula Two, for goodness' sake! — when his car left the track and hit a tree. He died instantly. 'No one knows why his car left the track,' says my dad.

No one ever knows why. I finish my breakfast. I take my bag. When the bus arrives, I make my way to school.

ALARM

The man is walking at a brisk pace. He walks with a slight limp; look closely, and you will see that the sole of his left shoe is worn down on its right-hand side, so that his foot lurches to the left every time it touches the ground. If this is painful, he gives no sign.

He is enjoying the weather and the view. The sun is shining steadily now, taking the chill off the persistent wind that blows over his shoulder. When he turns for a moment to look back up the hill, the wind blows his dark hair off his forehead, revealing a receding hairline. It's not easy to judge his age; some, citing the hair and the lines of worry that have settled in around his eyes, would place him in his early thirties; others would see the smooth, fleshy cheeks and the trace of adolescent gawkiness in his stride, and plump for the mid-twenties.

He stands there for quite a while, looking back; who

knows what he is thinking?

He turns and starts walking again. The smile returns to his face as he looks out over the park and the suburb stretched out below. He likes Newtown. You can gaze in the shop windows without feeling the pressure of hurrying suits that is always there in the central city, and it is the starting point for a host of potential expeditions: over to Hataitai, up to Mount Victoria, out to the zoo and then Island Bay. He's never been to Island Bay, and he wonders, as his gaze follows his thoughts, whether he can be bothered to go all the way out there today. It would probably take the best part of an hour to make it to the beach. He could find somewhere to have lunch, and wander back, and that would use up most of the day.

Of course, he could just have stayed at the house and sat and read, but he's sick of reading, and he's sick of that house. Only a day to go, but he wants to spend as little time there as possible. *What about tonight?* — the question is there all the time, but the sun is shining, and really, it's a hell of a view.

According to his map, that's Rugby League Park. Those seats look like they would be damn uncomfortable to sit on, but it's pleasant to imagine being part of a crowd, sitting there wrapped up in his jacket with maybe some sandwiches and a Thermos, if the weather is cold. He doesn't really know anybody who likes domestic rugby league, at least not enough to watch it live, but it would be okay to go along there on his own and get in behind the home team, whatever that is. The only Wellington team he knows about is Wainuiomata, but he's not keen enough to trek all the way out there just to see them.

Besides, he won't be here by Saturday afternoon.

You may as well know: he's just broken up with his girlfriend. That's what this is all about. It was so unexpected, too. He'd come up for the weekend and a couple of days either side, as they'd arranged, and he'd been looking forward to it, and Elaine said she'd been looking forward to it as well. She met him at the airport, same as usual, and they had dinner at her house, then went out to see a band. Wellington was notorious for its lack of proper venues; people were always starting up new places that ran for a year or so and then went bust or got closed down by the fire department. This was some place called the Loading Zone. They were early, and the band was late. The two of them sat at a table in the corner, ate nachos with cheese, beans and sour cream, and tried to talk, which was difficult with the noise from the jukebox and the people all around. He hated waiting for bands, and he wished they hadn't arrived so early.

Eventually the band appeared and started to play. They seemed pissed off, and played louder than usual, which with the terrible sound system meant that he was cast adrift in a great flood of noise that poured from the speakers and crashed against the bare concrete walls of the room.

Elaine towed him to the dance floor. He tried to locate the rhythm. She motioned him closer, and he put his arms on her shoulders. She was wearing that black lycra dress which, privately, he considered the sexiest item in her wardrobe. He ran his fingers over the faintly resistant fabric of the material. At the beginning of the next song, he bent down and put his hands around her waist, but she shook her head. Too restrictive. They danced apart after that. In the break before the encore, a rumour went round that the band had had a row with the promoter.

By the time they got home, they were both tired. He stank of smoke and wanted to wash the bitter smell off his body. When he emerged from the shower, she was already in bed and apparently asleep.

She had turned onto her side in her cotton nightdress. He moved across in the bed and put his arm across her belly, snuggling up close to her. He thought about moving his hand a little to cup her breast and stroke her nipple with his fingers, and felt a faint stir of arousal. But it was late, and they were both tired. He shifted a little, enjoying her warmth against his body, and drifted off to sleep.

By now he's made his way well down the hill, and is walking past the Winter Show Building, which he knows as the place where you play indoor cricket. If everything had gone according to plan, he might have started playing here regularly — in fact, they could both have been playing. He tried the men's grade a few years ago, when he was up here staying with some friends who played indoor, but it was too frantic for him. Also, that ball was bloody hard; he'd seen someone knocked out by it once, when they were fielding right near the back net. The mixed grade would have been the place for the two of them. He would have done quite well at that level.

Well, no sense worrying about that. He won't be playing here in a hurry. Not that he's about to abandon Wellington permanently — he likes the place, and he's got other friends here. But it would be good to take some time away, let some of the feelings settle down. Regret is the least productive of emotions.

He thinks he might walk down to the Basin Reserve. They spent a day there in summer, watching New Zealand play the Aussies. It was fine again (he's never understood why people complain so much about Wellington's weather), and they sat on the bank with some friends. He kept wanting to sit up to get a better view, but if you're not careful you slide down the hill and get your shorts up the crack in your bum. So he lay back on the blanket and talked about the game and drank two cans of beer and got a sunburned nose. Peter Taylor and Allan Border built up a long, slow partnership, but in the late afternoon New Zealand came back into the game, and by the close we were batting again. He and Elaine left the ground happy, and held hands as they made their way back up Adelaide Road and home for dinner. At the time, he was convinced they would always be together. Now, he peers at the grandstand in the distance and tries to take his mind off his troubles.

They had gone to see the band on Thursday night. On Friday morning, he was woken by her bloody alarm. It was a little pink thing with a 'snooze' setting, which meant it went off every five minutes and made snoozing impossible. Sometimes she set it for as early as 6am, but today, in deference to their late night, it went off at seven. She reached out a hand and squashed the alarm into submission, then rolled onto her side.

'Elaine, honey —' he said, and reached out his hand, which sometime during the night had slipped off her body and moved onto his own. He didn't care if it was just the effect of a full bladder; it was morning, he had an erection, and he wanted her. He moved closer to her and kissed the back of her neck, he touched the skin at the base of her buttock, just where the nightdress ended, and moved his hand upwards—

'No!' she said, and pushed him away. She got out of the bed without looking at him and headed off down the corridor. He lay back, wondering what he had done wrong. He hated when she was like this. He hated people being angry. What had he done? She'd been like this before, but she always came round in the end. Sometimes it took a while, though — and he was only here for a few days. Well, there was nothing you could say to her in this mood. Best to let it blow over. He would lie here for a while . . .

The alarm rang three more times before he summoned up the will to turn it off completely — it had an intricate little mechanism you had to think about, presumably to stop people turning it off in their sleep.

He got up and went into the kitchen. She was at the breakfast table. He said, how are you feeling? She told him she had decided their relationship wasn't working, and she wanted it to end. He said nothing. She said she didn't mind if he stayed for the rest of his time in Wellington, but after that, she didn't want to see him for a while. He said he'd try to get an earlier flight. He asked if there was someone else. She said, not yet. But she just didn't love him the way he loved her, and there was no point pretending. He said he really did love her, and that he didn't know what to say. She said, I know.

He sat there in silence. She said, come on, have some breakfast. He had some breakfast. She told him she was going to work. She said she was sorry. She gave him a hug. He duly hugged her back, but he couldn't feel her body in his arms.

When she had gone, he read the paper for a while. Nothing much was going on.

It looked like being a nice day. He rang the airline, who said they couldn't get a seat for him today, but they could get him back to Dunedin tomorrow if he was willing to pay forty dollars more. He said, okay. Then he went back and made the bed, and walked around the house for a bit, looking at things, like the two glasses he had bought so they could sit by the fire together and drink Drambuie and listen to music. Then he put on his jacket and headed out the door.

Now he's walked almost to the bottom of Adelaide Road, and he's trying to decide whether he wants to go and see the cricket museum at the Basin. He's heard there's some good stuff there — a bat used by Victor Trumper, a copy of the disc Bradman cut in England. The trouble is, going in there would remind him of happier times with Elaine. Everything reminds him of happier times. He'd be better off in the bush, by himself, with just the birds and the sandflies for company.

Somewhere down south, the sun is shining into a steep-sided valley that not a dozen people visit in a year. You get there by scrambling out of the lower valley before the gorge, then making your way along the tops just above the bushline. It's hot, and the scrub does cruel things to your sunburnt legs. Also, there isn't any water up there, and by the time the track drops down into the bush you're feeling the first flutterings of heat exhaustion. If you sit down for a while, that helps, and then you can make your way through the cool bush to the stream that flows along the edge of the flats. Take a drink, have a rest, then make your way across the flats, letting the long stems of grass make tiny scratches on your legs. The river flows in braided channels, and you can cross it if you're careful, one channel at a time. There's a rock by the far bank with a lawn of mosses and tiny grasses in front. Pitch your tent there. Dehydrating your dinner over the little stove, you can look out to the west and see the sun fall behind the jagged teeth of the peaks.

Dreaming of this inaccessible paradise, his feet decide against the cricket museum at the Basin. Watch him as he heads on down the street, around the ground, and into Cambridge Terrace. There are more people here, slower-moving than he, and he's forced to step around them. See him practise his sidestep. That woman with the shopping bags and the toddler is left for dead. He rounds the old man in the stained brown jacket and shapeless trousers with ease and sets off for a tryline that is always too far ahead. He is twenty-nine years old, and in his head still the boy who came home after school, polished off his homework and his dinner, and headed for the back yard to play ball by himself, setting up imaginary goalposts, choosing imaginary teams, keeping track as the score mounted and twilight flowed across the flat Southland plains.

He is lost here: send him back home. The tryline is too far ahead and the defenders are closing, their stronger legs carrying them across the turf. At any moment the tackles will come, and he will fall, his wind gone, the ball spilled. See him lie five yards short of the elusive white line, tears flowing from his eyes, pounding his fists in frustration into the damp, unyielding turf.

THE WADESTOWN SHORE

I cut the engine in the shadow of the motorway pillars and let the dinghy drift in to the Wadestown shore. The quiet of late afternoon was broken only by the squawking of parakeets. After locking the boat away in the old garage I now used as a boatshed, I stood for a moment to soak in the view. The setting sun was winking off the windows of drowned office blocks. To the left lay Miramar Island, and beyond it the open sea.

I turned from sea to hill and climbed the steps to the house, where Mum was sitting on the porch with a glass of wine in her hand.

'Pete strutting his stuff in the kitchen, is he?' I asked.

She nodded, her fair hair stirring against the collar of her jacket.

'Good, then I'll take his chair.' I swept it clear of his junk, then flopped down beside her. 'How was work?'

'Good. You?'

'Not bad. I went fishing among the office blocks.'

'Surely that's all been picked over by now?'

'You'd be surprised. The last time I was there, I dredged up a pair of gold earrings. Well worth the effort.'

'What did you get for them?'

'Fuel. And that book I gave you for your birthday.'

'And what did you find today?'

'Nothing much. Beats working in an office, though.'

She laughed. 'You're so like your father.'

It was true. I saw my father's features — dark hair, sharp nose — every time I looked in the mirror.

Our companionable silence was shattered by Pete. Everything about Pete was big: big belly, big voice, big opinion of himself.

'Grub's up!' he boomed. 'Hey, Stevie, my man! How's it hanging?'

'It's hanging fine, Pete. How about yours?'

'It's — hey, you're the sharp one, eh?' He raised both his hands, palms outwards, and made to slap mine. I kept my hands by my side.

I'll say one thing for Pete: he could cook. I wolfed down the lot, from the soup to the home-made ice cream, and even found room for a mango and a pawpaw from the orchard. I was too full to move after that, and I listened to Mum talk about her work. The Reconstruction Authority had extended its mandate for another two years, which bit the bippy of everyone at the Council because that meant another two years under the thumb of Taupo.

'Haven't we been Reconstructed enough?' I asked.

'According to Taupo, we're ninety per cent there, but it's that final ten per cent that always takes the longest.'

'They said we were ninety per cent there two years ago.'

'Steven, you know I don't like to hear you talking like that. You never know who could be listening.'

'Do you think they're bugging this house?'

'Steven!'

I subsided and let Pete tell us in great detail about his day in the garden shed. Him and his precious shed!

'Have you ever worked, Pete?'

'Sure I work. Look at these.'

'Yeah, I can see the grease under your fingernails. But I meant a job. For money.'

'Steven . . .' My mother had returned to Warning Level 1.

'No, no, Kate. Fair question. The boy's got a right to ask. So, Stevie, you think I should be earning my keep, eh?'

'The thought had crossed my mind.'

He looked downcast for a moment. 'I'd love to, son, I'd love to. And you'd think there'd be a need for professional meteorologists, but the Reconstruction Authority doesn't agree, and they pay the bills.'

'You could do something else,' I persisted.

'But there's no need for Peter to work, Steven. Say what you like about my job, it does pay well. Besides, your father worked from home, too.'

Until the night he woke up with his insides melting away.

We'd all got through the Drowning, that was the worst of it. I had been little more than a baby when the West Antarctic Ice Sheet began its graceful slide into the sea. Then the high tides came, higher every day until the new seawall failed and the water crashed in on streets and shops and houses. The new shoreline had more or less stabilised now, six metres above the old.

My father had told me all about it as he tinkered with flotsam and jetsam from pre-Drowning Wellington. In those days, it was all there for the taking along the new shoreline, and there was a thriving economy of scavenging and barter. When the shoreline had been picked clean, Dad acquired the dinghy. I spent as much time on that boat as I did at school, but I was in the classroom the day the principal came in and told us all to go straight home. New Variant Haemorrhagic Fever — the bleeding plague — had come to Wellington, and each household was thrown back on its own resources.

Just when we thought it had spared us, my father woke screaming in pain.

Ten days later, he lay buried in the orchard, and my mother and I were weak as newborn kittens but alive. When the plague had passed, she went back to work and I went back to school, but ours had become a silent house. I spent more and more time in Dad's workshop, tinkering with his pet projects, and stopped going to school altogether. When my mother found out, she was furious, and she hit me. I ran from the house and spent three nights living rough. I was as thin and wordless as a feral cat when I returned.

I moved into the workshop, and Mum didn't try to stop me. A photo of my father stood on the workbench beside my makeshift bed. I gazed at his dark, unsmiling face as if into a mirror.

I went back to school. Each day, when I got home, I would take Dad's boat out for a couple of hours' scavenging. I ate in the dark, alone, then did my homework with mechanical persistence. After a couple of months, I started talking to my mother again.

That was seven years ago. Ten months ago, ten long months, Pete came for dinner, and before I knew it he'd taken over the place — my father's boots, my father's chair, my mother's bed. I wouldn't let him have my dad's workshop, though.

'. . . Wouldn't you say, Stevie?'

Whatever inane question Pete had asked, he was waiting for an answer. 'Depends,' I said. 'Depends.'

'Damn, boy, you should move to Taupo and become a politician!' He laughed, his white teeth gleaming expensively. Pre-Drowning dental work, that. Everything had been better then.

I wrenched my attention back to the conversation. Mention of his old job had set Pete off, and he was deep into an explanation of why the summers were so much cloudier since the Drowning, why we got so few northerlies nowadays, and what had happened to the

Roaring Forties.

'So you're an amateur meteorologist these days, are you?'

The mask of bonhomie slipped for a moment, and he glared at me. 'No, I'm a professional meteorologist who's out of a job.' He smiled again. 'But yeah, I keep my hand in. You've got your workshop — I've got the garden shed. And I keep up, you know, on the Net.'

'So what have you got in the shed?'

'That's my business, boy.'

'I'll show you the workshop,' I offered.

He took the bait, though only after Mum nudged him. I flashed her a rueful smile and followed him to the shed. The interior was brightly lit — so that was where our power ration went — and crammed with paper, books, and electronics.

'Shit, what is all this stuff?' I asked as I stood in the doorway.

'This takes the readings from the anemometer — that little thing with the cups on the roof. This is a multimeter — hygrometer, barometer, thermometer and so on. I guess I am an amateur meteorologist at that, because I feed these readings in to the automated station over in Kelburn. Then over here I've got my GPS — you know what a GPS is, Stevie?'

'Can't say I do,' I lied.

'Global Positioning System receiver. Tells you exactly where you are on the planet. They were nearly as common as cellphones once.'

'Why aren't they common now?'

'The system depends on a bunch of satellites in low Earth orbit. Because they're so close to the top of the atmosphere, their orbits decay rapidly, and . . . am I boring you?'

'No, no, I'm interested.'

'Anyway, in the aftermath of the plague, new satellites weren't launched to replace those that burnt up, and the system crashed. It's only in the last couple of years they've got a workable system back up, although it's still nothing near what it used to be.' He picked up the receiver. 'These babies are pretty much restricted to Reconstruction Authority troops these days. I'm glad I hung on to this one.'

'Can I try it?'

'Sure.'

I pressed the touchpad, and a digital readout told me I was standing in the garden shed. 'Looks good to me,' I said. 'It sure would come in handy when I'm out in the dinghy.'

'Sorry, Stevie. Lose this overboard and I might never find another.'

'Okay.' I gave him a prospective-stepfather-grade smile. 'How about I show you the workshop tomorrow? Mum will be wondering where we are.'

Back at the house, Mum and Pete fell to reminiscing about old times. Pete was holding forth about the Drowning, about how ice cores had shown that this wasn't the first time that ice sheets had vanished in a few years, about how it could all change again just as quickly.

I would have to take my chances with that. I excused myself and went down to the workshop. I'd packed the previous night, but I opened my bags and went through it all again. If I forgot anything, there would be no second chance.

I said farewell to the many books I would have to leave behind, and once again went over the precious few I had decided to take. I straightened the pile of salvaged DVDs. I wrote a note for my mother. I prowled around the workshop, trying to decide whether any of my father's trinkets, as familiar and treasured as my mother's face, would be of use or ornament. I chose his compass. That might serve for both.

'Well, Dad,' I said to the empty air, 'I guess this is it. Someone else will get your stuff now. Maybe Pete will find a use for it. Hell of a waste if you ask me.'

I had waited long enough. I hefted my bag and closed the door for the last time.

Pete was snoring in their bedroom, and in the pauses between his snorts and gurgles I could hear my mother's softer breathing. Good. I tiptoed out into the garden and set to work. You don't make your living from the Drowned city centre without learning a thing or two about locks. I pocketed the GPS and all Pete's spare batteries and headed for the water's edge.

I didn't want to risk the motor, but soon realised I should have practised more with the oars. My back ached, and halfway to my destination I was forced to rest. I let the boat drift into the deeper shadow of the old railway station, between two wings, and slumped back for a few moments' rest.

A splash woke me. I was looking for its source when the boat rocked and someone began to haul themselves aboard. I reached for an oar and brought it down hard on the intruder's fingers. She cursed and let go. I was still off balance from the stroke when a second intruder pulled himself aboard, and it was all I could do to avoid toppling overboard. Then we were fighting at close quarters, wrestling in the bottom of the boat while it rocked in its own private storm.

My attention was divided between fighting off the intruder and trying to protect my precious gear. Before long, I was forced back against the bow, and when two hands seized my shoulders I knew I was done for. I slumped in fear and frustration, and it saved me: I felt the blade of the other oar against my hand. I smashed it into my assailant's groin and, before he could recover, used the oar to lever him off the boat. Then I hit him on the head. There was no sign of the woman.

Shivering, I fumbled with the outboard. The motor caught, and I made my way out of the artificial bay, skimming over abandoned platforms. There were lights, shouts, and the splash of something heavy hitting the water behind me, but I ignored them. When I judged I was safe, I pointed the boat in the right direction, cut the motor, and took stock.

If the motive was robbery, my assailants weren't very

good at it, because the only thing missing was one of the oars. My bag was intact, but the GPS had slipped into the bilgewater. Heart pounding, I picked it up, shook it gently, and pressed the touchpad. It worked! Praise the Lord and pre-Drowning technology. I packed it into my bag, restarted the engine, and hurried onwards.

I was over the old harbour now, the Drowned towers behind me, their windows as dark and featureless as their walls. I would leave their remaining secrets for others to discover. I was sick of them, sick of the whole place, mired in regret for its glorious, irretrievable past. It was time to move on.

Before me, my destination loomed just as dark: Te Papa was our place now. Years ago, the glass of the second-floor windows had been removed, and now the cavernous space within made a fine boat harbour, its gloom shrouding our comings and goings. The outboard motor was loud between the echoing walls, but I had what we needed, so that no longer mattered.

I was met by Losi and Trey. Losi opened her mouth to tear a strip off me for being late, but I forestalled her by offering up the GPS. 'I had to fight to get it here,' I said. 'The least you could do is be grateful.'

That shut them up. I followed them up the stairs and across to the other side of the building. They let down the rope ladder, and there she was, enjoying her first night out on the open waters for almost two years. 'She looks great,' I said. Losi glared at me and reminded me about the correct use of pronouns.

The *Tangaroa* was a cruising yacht that had capsized during the Drowning and lost much of its gear. Trey's father had acquired the yacht in one of his many deals, and Trey inherited it when the old man died. His father had used it as a diving platform, but Trey wasn't interested in diving. He had a longer trip in mind. One night, he took down its masts and manoeuvred the *Tangaroa* into the gutted museum.

So he had a vessel. While searching for an engineer, he met Losi, and found himself a partner as well. Word reached me that there was a crazy American looking for people with a sense of adventure and a desire to leave their past behind. He needed my knowledge of the waterfront and the equipment that could be scavenged there, so he took me on and told me to learn all I could about weather and currents. Slowly, the project took shape. Replacing the electronic equipment had been the hardest part. We relied on Kiwi ingenuity and outright theft for that.

The three of us stood in the cabin and looked at the GPS. 'It's not very big,' Losi said. 'Are you sure it will do the job?'

'I'm as sure of that as you are of the hull.'

Losi scowled at me. She'd sworn up and down that the hull would cope with anything the Southern Ocean could throw at it. Some of us weren't so confident, but there was nothing we could do about that now.

Food was going to be the other big challenge. We'd installed fishing gear, and our precious cargo of seeds and embryos was tucked safely in the freezers. The cold-tolerant hybrids Belinda had acquired for us would soon be needed.

Everything was packed. By dawn, all twelve of us were aboard. There was no point hanging around. Silently, we cast off, and *Tangaroa* eased its way into the light.

It was a beautiful morning in balmy Wellington. The boat slipped through the crystal waters. The faces of my crewmates, pale from working in the darkness, blossomed in the sun. We chose the eastern exit from the harbour; boats attempting the western route were all too likely to snag on the Drowned houses of Lyall Bay. As we slipped past Eastbourne, the scent of freedom filled my nostrils. Under way at last!

The southern tip of Miramar Island passed to starboard, its dark green foliage dappled with light by the sun, while to port, tall grey turbines ran down the ridge to Pencarrow Head. We were about to reach the open water, where my knowledge of wind and tide would be put to the test.

Just before we hit the swells of the open sea, I took a last look back. Had Mum found my note yet? I would call her when I could, if I could, if the radio worked when we got there.

The sunken office blocks of the Drowned city were far behind me. The rich waters and virgin shores of Antarctica lay ahead. I made my way forward to greet them.

FILLING THE ISLES

It was good in the old days. Claire — that's Kevin and our Sarah's Claire — could see us most days, and she'd wave and smile. She was such a friendly girl. But then they moved to the other side of the hill, and that was the last we saw of them. Neighbours are all right, but it's not the same as family, is it? That's why I'm so glad to see you.

Isn't it a lovely view? You can see all the way to the McKinnons'; well, George anyway, he's taller than Diana. You can just make out her hair if you look carefully. They're where the cellphone tower used to be, until it was taken down. I miss being able to call everybody. Now we can only talk to our neighbours if everyone else is quiet. And that doesn't happen very often!

How far did you say you came? Three hundred people? That must have taken you a while.

I hope you didn't have any trouble with the neighbours.

Some of them might think you were going to take their space. I told them you were just coming for a visit when I saw you, but—

Oh, is that right? Well, dear, Mr Chen might be a bit grumpy, but as I tell him, the good Lord made room enough for all His children, and we should too. We can always squeeze in one more.

Put your foot there, dear, that will make a bit more space.

I do like being on top of a hill. You feel the wind a bit more, especially when it blows from the south, but on the other hand you get your food and water before everyone down in the valleys, and it's less likely those embarrassing bags will get dropped when you hand them over to the clean-up team.

Do you think the food's getting better or worse? I think the food's getting better. I'm sure it is.

We have an agreement on this hilltop that if a new person comes, or someone moves out or passes on — like poor Mrs Masters, dear, who died just the other day, a frail wee thing she was at the best of times — then the ones who've been here the longest get the first chance to change where they stand and when they sleep. And if I could just offer you a word of advice, dear, it's to make sure you don't end up sleeping next to that young man over there, that Rory Wilson. I don't need to tell you why, do I, dear? You're old enough to know.

Of course, you young people do what you like nowadays. There was one young couple, standing just over there, who were no better than animals. Do you remember animals? We had a lovely rat when I was young. Anyway, this couple wouldn't listen even when we told them to stop, so we squeezed them out. We had to. It wasn't right. If you do find yourself a young man, dear, you and he have got to wait till the people around you are sleeping. You'll usually find that something can be arranged.

Brrr, that wind is cold. I don't like the look of those clouds, either. I don't mind a bit of rain — we've all got our coats, after all — but what I hate is standing in the clouds. You can catch your death that way. I've seen whole hillsides of bodies after a few days stuck in the mist. They should put the young men on the high mountains, in my opinion. It's not right to send mothers with young babies up there. I try to tell them that, but they just smile at me and tell me not to worry.

Well, dear, it's almost my sleeping time. When I wake up, I'll have a talk to the neighbours and we'll fit you in to the sleeping roster. You're welcome to stay here as long as you like; I'd be glad of the company. But if you do want to leave, take my advice: head back north. See that hilltop to the south? I wouldn't want to be standing there, because it's very steep on the far side, and after that, there's only the sea.

HOMESTAY

We skimmed out of the clouds just above the mountains. 'Mount Isolation,' I informed my companions. 'Access Peak. Grave-Talbot Pass.'

'Look at me,' said Jacques. 'I'm a mountain parrot!' He flew in tight circles around us, cawing loudly.

'That parrot needs a perch,' said Kevin. 'How about there?' He pointed up the valley to the wall of rock at its head.

'Homer Saddle,' I said, my little voice still faithfully feeding me the names.

We levelled out, Jacques clowning around us, and flew the length of the valley in formation.

Kevin reached the rock wall first. He stretched his wings to their fullest extent and dropped gracefully onto the far edge of the narrow saddle. Nicola and I joined him on either side, and with much preening of imaginary feathers, Jacques joined us too, hopping from foot to foot.

'I need to go,' he said.

We watched the stream of urine arc over the edge of the saddle, catch in the updraft, and fly up again, thoroughly wetting Jacques's bodysuit. When we stopped laughing, I told Jacques he should find a lake to wash in. 'There's one to the south, Lake Thompson,' I said. He took off at once.

'Think we should follow him? The water will be very cold.'

'I'm sick of that idiot already,' said Kevin. 'A few minutes without him would be bliss.' So we sat and watched him dwindle among the mountains.

When Jacques reappeared from his dip, he was swooping in a way that was either a poor imitation of his beloved mountain parrot or the sign of a flyer in trouble. 'Jacques, are you—'

Too late. Jacques was closing fast, but in no controlled way. One wing hung limply. He rose in the air, called something in exaltation or despair, and plummeted, smashing headfirst into the granite wall some 200 metres below us. He bounced off the rocks and fell straight to the base of the cliff, landing in a jumble of rocks near the southern tunnel entrance, where the old road emerged from the darkness.

We flew down and looked at him. He was broken.

'I told you he was an idiot,' said Kevin.

'Well,' shrugged Nicola, 'at least he had his fun.'

We'd had enough adventure for one day. We left Jacques where he lay and flew south to find shelter.

We spent the night in the dubious refuge of an abandoned cabin at Te Anau Downs. There was no food, and these bodies needed food. To feel hunger was interesting.

Morning. It is always cold here! Nicola was all for pressing on to Invercargill, but neither Kevin nor I felt quite ready to tackle such a big city. We settled for a leisurely flight across country, following the scarcely used roads. In the early afternoon, we found a café still open in a town that clung on where two roads met. Though we furled our wings tightly before we entered, the woman behind the counter (the first downsider we had encountered at close range) looked at us with deep suspicion. But when Nicola put money — actual physical coins — on the counter, she gave us what we asked for.

So this was how our ancestors ate! Not on the wing, of course.

'This stuff is toxic,' I said, forcing down a green, ill-flavoured mouthful.

'Of course,' said Kevin. 'That's why they die.'

Towards evening, muscles pleasantly weary, we flew down a line of hills towards the largest town we had seen thus far.

'Gore,' said Nicola, forestalling me. 'Let's avoid it.'

'So where will we sleep tonight?'

'Homestay.' She waited for her little voice. 'Many farms derived extra income from taking in travellers on a per-night or per-week basis. Some encouraged guests to take an active part in farm life. Accommodation was typically in quarters built for farmhands whom the farm no longer needed to employ.'

Just off the main highway and short of the town, we found a compound that appeared to meet our requirements. Kevin wanted to buzz the sheds and outhouses, but wiser counsel — that is to say, mine — prevailed, and we landed a few hundred metres up the road, then puffed and stumped towards the farmyard.

Before we entered the driveway, we checked that our wings were so tightly furled as to look no more than ridges of muscle on our backs, and critiqued the colours we had chosen for our bodysuits, each as close to natural fabrics — shaggy things like wool and cotton — as we could make them. Our supply of coins was not limitless, and doubtless, the more bizarre we looked, the more we would have to pay for our accommodation.

Kevin took the lead as we crunched up the driveway, and knocked first. The door was opened by a woman and a dog; I presume the woman turned the handle, but the dog leapt in front of her, growling ferociously. Its hackles rose as it met my gaze.

'What do you want?' the woman asked above the din.

'We are travellers who seek a room for a night, and perhaps longer,' I said. 'We have money.'

'You're not from around here.'

'We are tourists.'

'A long while since we've seen any of those.'

There was nothing I could say to that. We waited while the woman looked us over and the dog growled.

'Harv!' she called.

A man joined her in the doorway. He was large.

'What do you want?'

'We are travellers who seek a room for a night, and perhaps longer,' I told him. 'We have money. Will you keep us standing on your doorstep all night?'

'Guess not,' said the man. 'Come in.'

We filed past the dog into a room filled with shapes and noise, too much to take in all at once. Three extra places were found at the table. Nicola and the woman talked, and money changed hands. The woman led us from the table, down a long corridor, and across a yard to a bunk room that lay empty. It was very cold, but she found a heater and switched it on. There were four bunks; this reminded me of Jacques.

Then back to the dining room for food and conversation. The food was a mixture of warm things in a thick sauce, very tasty and filling. The conversation mostly proceeded between the inhabitants of the farm: the older couple we had met at the door, various sons and daughters and relatives, and workers who were, in many cases, also relatives or daughters or sons.

'It is a complex kinship network,' Nicola whispered to me.

'Why are there so many of them?'

'Let me see. Ah. Following the oil depletion crisis of

the early twenty-first century, farms could no longer rely on the internal combustion engine for transport energy. They were forced to revert to human and animal muscle power for many tasks.'

'Tell us something about yourselves,' said Harv McKenzie, leaning towards us. 'Where are you from?'

'We are from Germany,' I said. It was not entirely false. 'We are on a flying holiday.'

'There's not many people can afford to fly any more,' said Harv.

'We are quite rich,' I explained.

'So where's your airship, or whatever you're using?' asked a woman across the table.

'We don't need those,' said Kevin, 'because we have these.' He stood and unfurled his wings.

Those on Kevin's side of the table scrambled out of the way. Voices were raised in shock and outrage, mine among them. Kevin's wings reached almost the length of the room, and stood iridescent in the buttery light, defying easy explanation.

'What the hell are those?' asked Harv.

'Isn't that obvious? They're wings.'

'Yeah, but what are they made out of?'

'A nanotubule matrix bonded with . . .' I had never troubled myself with such details, but Kevin was young enough to delight in showing off his — or rather his little voice's — technical knowledge. Before long he was persuaded to lead a party of the easily impressed outside to show them his wings in action. Adulation at a stroke: he would be in his element here.

Nicola and I were also questioned, and admitted that yes, we too had wings, but that we preferred to open them only when needed for flight.

'Or in private,' added Nicola. Her gaze swept the room as she said it, and I saw male gazes linger in return.

The thirst for new experience is universal. Neither Kevin nor Nicola slept in our quarters that night.

I was woken deep into the night by a knock on the door. 'Who is it?' I managed, still surfacing from the unfamiliar depths of sleep.

A female voice. 'I was wondering . . .'

It was the woman who had opened the door to us. Her skin as I caressed it was pitted and cracked, roughened by time and use. On the narrow and uncertain surface of the bunk, I folded her in my wings, and we made love until light leached into the morning sky.

The next few days passed pleasantly enough. When we were not satisfying the questions and the desires of our acolytes, we flew sorties over the neighbouring hills, or did our comical best to help around the farm. As we did so, my contempt for these dwellers in the flesh was replaced, or at least moderated, by admiration: they did so much with so little!

Topside, we thought of the ground-dwellers, if we thought of them at all, as scrabbling and dying in a sea of blood, mud, and poverty. But here, though they surely had the mud — we had to wash it off each other's wings before we took flight — they had made some kind of life for themselves. Their land would grow many crops if they treated it well, and they now had no choice but to do so. Though most work had to be done by horse or by hand, they grew enough food to feed themselves and produce a surplus.

Saturday was market day. The horses' breath sent clouds of steam into the dawn air as, hoof by careful hoof, they eased the farm's wagons down the hill that led into the town.

Gore: blood, also a triangle of land. The market was held on that triangular common, next to the river. Our stall had been erected in advance, and soon it was filled with the finest of the week's produce. Locals squelched through the mud and the horseshit, bargaining for this and bartering for that.

We attracted much attention. 'Show us your wings, mister!' pleaded a small boy. I stared at him until his father, somewhere between apology and truculence, took him by the hand and dragged him away. A crowd of the curious and the scandalised gathered to gossip and point. But those who came to gawk stayed to buy, and the stall did good business.

I was wondering when we'd break for breakfast, or lunch, when Cousin Amy came running up to us, her face distraught. 'Come quickly, it's Kevin . . .'

Physical labour had limited appeal to Kevin. He had found his way to the nearest tavern and got himself shamefully drunk with young men of a similar disposition. They had dared him to show them his flying prowess, and now he was trying to oblige.

'I', he called from the top of a clock tower, 'can fly! Look at this!'

He performed a drunken circuit above the upturned faces below, barely regaining his footing as he landed.

I was still hesitating when Nicola took off from the edge of the crowd. Kevin took this as a challenge.

'This silly cow thinks she's a better flyer than me! Think again!'

Kevin, being Kevin, had chosen wings optimised for maximum power rather than maximum control when he specified his body for our downside adventure. Though he was weaving all over the sky, and Nicola was taking a dead straight line after him, he still outraced her. By now, I too was in the air, watching as Kevin swooped low over the river. I saw the tip of one wing catch the top of a wave. He dipped dangerously towards the water, recovered, and raced under the twin bridges that linked the west and east sides of town.

The rich Southland soil produced more than even market day could absorb, and it was all transported by electric train, north to Dunedin, south to Invercargill. It was the northbound train that hissed onto the rail bridge as Kevin flew under it, and it was the northbound train that caught him a glancing blow as he flew up from beneath the bridge, preparing to loop the loop. He disappeared under the wagons.

From death to funeral took a long time. The local coroner insisted on an inquest, primarily, I suspect, to satisfy his curiosity about this winged apparition. I offered my help, but he declined it. A proud man, the coroner.

A verdict of accidental death was returned. At the funeral, I was asked to say a few words.

'Kevin was my friend,' I began. 'He enjoyed his sojourn in your world very much. Sadly, he left this world too soon. He has gone where we all must go, and I will see him there myself in due course. I hope and believe that he is happy there.'

This went down very well, and Nicola congratulated me later.

And now we were two. I cannot say that I missed either Kevin or Jacques greatly as individuals, but I began to feel lonely now both of them were gone. Hannah McKenzie had stopped coming to my bed after Kevin died, and would not tell me why; her husband treated me with the same bluff good humour as before, so it did not seem that he had discovered us. I was beginning to feel less like a tourist and more like a member of the household, but I did not want to spend the rest of my downside days on a farm.

While Kevin spread his favours widely among the young women of the farm, Nicola had taken up with a sturdy young man called Bill. One night, she came to me instead of him. I awoke, warm and sleepy, to see her bending over me.

'I want to stay here,' she said. 'I want to have a baby.'

'Can you have a baby?'

'I don't see why not. This body is fully functional.'

'But what about your work back home?'

'What about it? Reactivate my consciousness when you get back.'

'But then you — this you — can never return.' (It was our law that only one instance of each consciousness could exist in our polity.)

She made a face. 'I'm sick of it. The perfect weather, the perfect lives, the perfect endless happiness. I prefer this world, the real world, where things get old and die. I want you to cut off my wings.'

I mouthed incomprehension.

'Have you looked in the mirror lately? Spread out your wings and look carefully.'

In the light from the yellow bulb, I saw that she was right. When the probe had dropped us below the tropopause and we flexed our wings for the first time, we had thought them indestructible. But they were beginning to fray at the edges from the heavy air and hard uses of this world, and down here we had no way to repair them.

'As long as I have them,' said Nicola, 'there'll be the temptation to fly away. Cut them off.'

'Does Bill agree?'

'He doesn't know.'

As she knelt in front of me in that narrow room, I felt an overwhelming urge to possess her; overwhelming, but futile, since she would no longer have me. How marvellous it had been to feel our wings beat together on our first night! And now she would rather stay with a man whose life could be measured in years.

Working with care and without undue haste, I cut along the lines of attachment between her wings and her back.

'You'll still feel the urge to flex them from time to time,' I warned her; then, 'Don't shrug. I don't want to slice through your flesh.'

Next morning, I rose early and went outside. The autumn was deepening towards winter. The ground was cold beneath my boots as I dug. In went Nicola's wings, then I filled the hole up again, and took off my boots.

It was almost dawn. Soon the farm would be rising. I removed my farm clothes and sprang into the air in the brightly coloured flying suit that had brought me here. So good, to be free again! Soon I would awake in my familiar world, a consciousness inside a computer in a European Space Agency satellite launched seventeen years earlier from Guyana, in that final brief flowering before the oil ran out and the world ran down. There we made the things of the mind, and our machines carried out our desires.

Up I flew, and the sun splashed across me as I rose into the dawn. I let out a great shout, swooping and diving in the photon wind. This, I would miss; this, and the ground spread out like a banquet below me. Up. I would not reactivate Nicola's consciousness when I returned. She would surely tire of her life on the farm before long, and end it, and so return to her real life, topside.

Up again, and now the air was too cold and too thin to sustain me. My thoughts dove away from me, and my body tumbled after them. An impact, a brief moment of blackness, then I awoke in my own world. Kevin and Jacques were there to greet me, and we spoke from mind to mind, and walked out together under the perfect, illusory sky.

THE VISIT OF M. FOUCAULT TO HIS BROTHER WAYNE

At the saleyards, M. Foucault was impressed by the auctioneer, the cattle, the long, dark-brown coats and wide-brimmed hats, the interplay of *langue* and *parole*. Wayne bought two steers and a heifer. The Douglas brothers, who farmed down Edendale way, entered into the zero of the signified, and made a loss.

On the way back to 'Dunroamin', Wayne expounded upon the difficulties facing the rural intellectual. The local Fed Farmers had knocked his ideas back several times, and they just plain wouldn't listen any more. M. Foucault reflected upon the discourse of marginalisation, and embraced his brother before they re-entered the homestead.

That night, Wayne and Shirl had a few of the neighbours around to meet the visiting celebrity. There were lamingtons. The neighbours asked, 'So what do you do for a crust?' and 'What do you reckon to that Bernard Laporte?' and 'What's so bad about prisons, anyway?' The last of them left by 9.30pm, as there was milking to be done in the morning. M. Foucault helped Shirl with the dishes. He tried to be, how do you say, a good bloke.

Smoking a Gauloise and shivering, M. Foucault leant on the veranda rail and looked at the stars, now revealed, now occluded by scurrying wisps of cloud. He imagined himself to be on the Left Bank. A ute drove past on the road to Mandeville, and the dogs in their low-roofed cages began to bark. M. Foucault ducked back inside and sought the comfort of his books.

At haymaking, at feeding out, in spring when the creek flooded and they had to rescue twenty sheep by dinghy from under the macrocarpas, M. Foucault felt himself to be like a spare wheel. 'You're like a spare wheel,' said Wayne, without rancour.

Only at milking did M. Foucault excel. 'You've got nice hands,' said Shirl, and it was true: the cows seemed to appreciate his attentions, whereas, with Wayne, it was always a battle of man against beast. Seeing the milk in the churn, making deliveries to the dairy factory in Mataura, M. Foucault felt an unmediated glow of satisfaction.

On the night he returned to Paris, his friends celebrated with a restaurant dinner. Lacan and Kristeva had Big Macs and Baudrillard a Quarter Pounder. 'They fed me well on the flight,' said M. Foucault, contenting himself with a large fries and a shake. He ate without tasting, recalling a system of signs that directed traffic to its appropriate destination along gravel roads, a hegemony of sausage rolls and the Ladies' Excuse-Me.

'Look at him,' said Baudrillard, 'he's off his food.' But Baudrillard had always been envious, and the others only smiled fondly at their friend and mentor, and made mental notes to enquire later if, perhaps, there might be a professorial vacancy in the Collège de France before long.

BORGES AND I

Borges comes round with a six-pack just in time for the game. I tell him he could have got it cheaper down the road. He nods unhappily, as is his way.

Half-time, and the ABs have had a shocker. Borges, of course, has divided loyalties; he says he'll be happy if Argentina lose by less than twenty points, or the All Blacks win by more than fifty. I tell him I need to go for a piss. Two Exports will do that to anyone.

When I get back, Borges is making himself a coffee. Is it possible, he asks me, that Amphixion of Thebes was thinking of rugby when he wrote that each game played by men is one moment of the game played by the gods?

I tell him he'd better get back to the couch if he wants to see the second half, and besides, only woofters drink coffee at half-time.

The All Blacks win 42–17. Sevens against Thebes? It's possible.

Borges and I go out for a few quiets. I meet him after work in a bar favoured by web developers and business analysts. We sit and watch a small subset of the world go by.

Borges looks glum. 'Bad day in the stacks?' I ask. He nods, says nothing, swallows another mouthful of beer.

I nudge him. 'Look, over there. I happen to know those women are studying to be librarians. Go and dazzle them with your learning. That's what it's for, man!'

He surprises me by draining his glass and walking right up to them. Asks them a question; they look surprised, but make room for him. He turns and waves me over.

'This is Brian,' he says. 'He's something in computers.'

Borges talks to the dark one, I talk to the fair. She's a bit serious for me. Nothing doing there, but Borges and Krystal are getting on like a house on fire — so well that I say my goodbyes and walk home under the indifferent dome of eternity. Borges, eh? You never would have thought it.

Borges and I scarcely see each other nowadays. What with his work and the kid, Borges is too damned busy, and besides, all he wants to talk about is how little Pedro took two steps the other day, how Pedro looked at him and said 'Mama', how when Pedro wakes in the night Borges walks him round the house till the little fella settles back down. The bookcases have survived from his old flat, but now they're full of *Your Baby and Child* and *Raising Boys*.

'So where are your old books?' I ask him after the grand tour. (Krystal is at yoga.)

'Out the back, in suitcases. Want to borrow them?'

'Choose me an armful.'

They aren't easy going, those books, but I've learned (from passages underlined by Borges) that Goncalves compared eternity to a mirrored sphere, while Basilides was exiled from Mount Athos for teaching that the world would end when the souls of the elect called God to account for human suffering. It seems to me sometimes, as I wake on my couch to find the wisdom of ages in unsteady piles around me, that the world will end when there is no longer room for all the books in it; but when I suggested this to Borges, he said he had less than four hours' sleep last night and a meeting of the Library Board next morning, and could I call him later?

I have moved into Borges' former apartment. It was renovated after Borges moved out, but with heavy drapes across the windows and the lighting turned down low I don't notice the difference. How I miss those days when we'd lounge around discussing the pre-Socratics and Cameron Diaz! Back then, I used to tease him that he should get out more. Well, he did, and it landed him two kids and a house in the suburbs.

Having quit my job in computers, I am living on my savings. I have decided to become a writer. Borges, informed of this, sighs and tells me I should get a life.

MEASURELESS TO MAN

Exmoor, England, 1797

In Xanadu did Kubla Khan
a half-day holiday decree . . .

Samuel Taylor Coleridge frowned. He was damned if he could get this poem right. In his latest laudanum-induced stupor, he had dreamed up some vague, fantastical picture of mythical kings and flowing rivers, but he could get no further than the opening couplet. Crumpled scraps of paper were strewn across the floor; he had even hurled one or two out the window. He scratched out this latest effort and set to work again.

In Xanadu did Kubla Khan
a block of council flats decree . . .

No, that wasn't it either. Botheration and befogglement! The poet threw down his pen, stretched . . .

And heard a knock at the door. Blast you, he thought, waiting to see if the intruder would go away. The knock was repeated. Coleridge cursed sulphurously; he hated being interrupted during one of his muse's unpredictable visits. A third knocking, louder this time; the wretch was determined. Block of council flats — what could that possibly mean? Still shaking his head, he set off for the door.

Dawdling down the passage, thinking of ways to fob off the visitor, he realised who it must be: Joanna Siddeley, daughter of the local squire, whom he had been browbeaten into accepting for instruction in poesy.

Coleridge regarded himself as a free thinker, but he was not convinced of the propriety of women writing. Joanna's father had made much the same point as he paced up and down before Coleridge's fireplace, soiling the poet's one good carpet with his mud-encrusted boots.

'Not sure I approve of a filly writing, you know — damned dubious profession, writing, if you'll pardon my opinion, present company excepted of course, or perhaps not, from what they say in the village, eh?' The squire leered significantly at Coleridge. Coleridge, who had no idea what he was on about, nodded cautiously.

'But the thing is, she's got her heart set on it. Wants to be another Shakespeare, she does, or that poet chappie — what's his name — friend of yours—'

'Wordsworth,' interjected Coleridge glumly. That, it seemed, was to be his fate. Wordsworth's friend. A minor member of the Wordsworth school. Dear, sweet William. Well, Mr Philistine, let me tell you—

'That's the cove. Well, I thought, what the deuce, it won't hurt her and you look like you could do with the money, what?'

'About the money—'

'But mark my words, young man,' said the squire, thrusting his choleric face close to Coleridge's melancholy one, 'no funny business, eh? She's a damned fine-looking filly, if I say so myself, and she ought to make a damned good match with Viscount Hawker's lad. I know you poet chappies — not above having your way with a blushing virgin, eh? Well, sir, save your attentions for the village girls, and leave my daughter alone, d'ye hear?'

Coleridge heard. Not a problem, he thought, envisaging a braying daughter of the aristocracy, more horse than woman. 'Getting back to the money, Squire Siddeley . . .'

When Coleridge opened the door, the first sight of Joanna Siddeley drove all thought of Xanadu from his mind. She was a beauty, tall and stately, with infinitely green eyes and an expression of cool amusement. There was a clearing of throats, and an older, plainer woman interposed herself between Coleridge and the fair Joanna.

'I'm here to make sure that everything is . . . acceptable,' the chaperone proclaimed.

'Acceptable?'

'Above board,' said the woman firmly. 'My name is Parsons. I am Miss Siddeley's governess.'

'Come in, come in, Miss Siddeley . . . Miss Parsons?'

'Mrs Parsons. My husband attends to the squire's stables.'

'Very malodorous of him, I'm sure. Sit down, Miss Siddeley, and you over here, Mrs Parsons.' He carefully placed Mrs Parsons behind him, so that he could fix his gaze on the perfection of Joanna's face. 'Now, my dear, do you have anything to show me?'

One of Joanna's eyebrows lifted fractionally. Coleridge, realising what he had said, blushed. He coughed unconvincingly and covered his embarrassment with a handkerchief. 'That is, have you brought any samples of your writing?'

'Certainly, Mr Coleridge. Perhaps you'd care to cast an eye over these.' She drew a sheaf of poems from her bag and handed them over.

And they were good. Very good. Coleridge was astounded that the daughter of a country squire should be able to write so well and so convincingly about subjects normally thought the province of men of affairs. There were, perhaps, some rough edges, some small infelicities, but the overall standard was remarkable. He read them in silence, handed them back to her, and paused to collect his thoughts.

'Well, Mr Coleridge, what do you think?'

He looked at her to deliver his reply and found himself

staring straight into those eyes. There was something hypnotic about them, something— He pulled himself together with an effort, his mind awaiting the return of its blood supply.

'I . . . er . . . that is, that is, I'm impressed! Very impressed. These are wonderful poems, Miss Siddeley. You have a fine style, a strong imagination, what I might call a "numinous air" about your work. If I can dare a criticism, it is that there are, perhaps, some turns of phrase and expression which any potential audience might find a little . . . unseemly, coming from a woman?'

Her face darkened. 'Mr Coleridge, if I wish to be patronised I have my father close at hand. It is your job to suggest improvements in my poetry, not to weaken it by appeals to the taste of an imagined audience. If any readership I may acquire is as easily shocked as you suggest, why then, I will publish under a male pseudonym until such attitudes are left behind. Now, shall we proceed?'

'Very well, Miss Siddeley, very well.'

They worked steadily for the next hour, Coleridge suggesting changes, Joanna accepting or rejecting them. They were interrupted by Mrs Parsons, who had been engaged in silent and unnoticed chaperonage somewhere in the recesses of the room. 'Time we were getting back, Miss Joanna.'

Two heads, bowed over the paper to consider a particularly complex metaphor, straightened regretfully. Joanna smiled, and Samuel's heartstrings executed a pizzicato passage. 'Same time next week, Miss Siddeley?'

'Same time next week, Mr Coleridge. But, before I go, I found this outside.' She produced a crumpled sheet of paper, straightened it, read it out.

> *In Xanadu did Kubla Khan*
> *Consume an extra cup of tea*

'An early draft, my dear, nothing to take too seriously. Just a little thing I've been working on.'

'I took it upon myself to pen a few alternative lines as we waited at your door. What do you think of these?'

> *In Xanadu did Kubla Khan*
> *A stately pleasure dome decree*
> *Where Alph, the sacred river, ran*
> *Through caverns measureless to man*
> *Down to a sunless sea*

Coleridge stared at Joanna's lines in astonishment. They were perfect: just what he'd been groping dimly towards. How wonderful! How humiliating!

'Hmmmm, yes, that's not a bad effort, not a bad effort at all. I'd done quite a bit more work on it by the time you arrived, of course, so I've got some ideas of my own, but I'll certainly bear this in mind. Thank you, my dear, and we'll meet again next week.'

Coleridge escorted the pair to the door, then returned to ponder the poem. That was what he was after, no doubt about it — and the damned woman had beaten him to it! Of course, no one could say it was her idea. The whole concept was his; she had merely embellished it.

Just the way Wordsworth keeps taking my ideas, 'embellishing' them, and publishing the resulting poems as his own?

Well, yes . . . but he gets away with it, doesn't he?

And she's only a slip of a girl. Who'd believe she could have thought this up by herself? I'd be doing her a favour by publishing the thing under my name.

All for the best, really.

Rationalisation having triumphed over conscience, he set to work to complete the poem. He had penned another forty-nine lines by the time Joanna was due to arrive for her second lesson, and was wondering whether to show them to her. Being a forward sort of girl, she might demand attribution, and that wouldn't do at all. What if his wife found out?

The clock ticked on past 2pm, but Joanna did not arrive. Coleridge tried to return to his literary endeavours, but felt unsettled. Where could she be? He wanted to see her — he *needed* to see her.

The knock on the door came at quarter to three. Coleridge sprang up, flung the door open — and was met by the disapproving gaze of Mrs Parsons.

'What's happened? Where's Joanna?'

'Miss Siddeley to you, sir, and she won't be coming today, nor any other day for that matter.'

'Why on earth not? She was so full of promise!'

Mrs Parsons's mouth made a bow of disapproval. 'Well, sir, from now on her promise will be reserved exclusively for Viscount Hawker. When I advised the squire of some of the things that had passed between the two of you, sir, and in particular of Miss Joanna's remarks concerning himself, he waxed quite wroth, and ordered the young Viscount to propose to Miss Joanna at once. He arrived by carriage in the middle of the night and went to her on bended knee, and they're to be married in the spring.'

'How much say did she have in the matter?'

'Miss Joanna knows her duty, sir, and if she doesn't there are those of us obliged to point it out to her. The squire has instructed me to pay you for your time last week, and for this week as well — you'll find it's all there, sir — and to inform you that if he sees you sniffing round his daughter again he'll pin you to your front door by your organ of benevolence, sir.'

'Vindictive cow,' muttered Coleridge.

'That's as may be, sir, but I know my place when there's those as don't.' Mrs Parsons's face softened for a moment. 'She's a fine young woman, though, isn't she, sir? You'll not be the only one disappointed to see her go.'

Gathering her skirts and her disapproving air around her once more, Mrs Parsons trudged back the way she had come.

Coleridge was stunned, and had to prepare a double dose of laudanum to calm himself. Wild scenarios whirled through his head: a personal plea to the squire or to Viscount Hawker . . . a deputation of poets to rescue her . . . a kidnapping, by Jove, and romantic moonlit pursuit! Upon reflection, each plan seemed to combine a remote chance of success with a high degree of risk to his — Samuel Taylor Coleridge's — life, health, or reputation.

By the next day, he had come to terms with the situation. It was the way of the world: women must weep . . . and men must work. He drew out his manuscript and began to consider what should follow the lines

> *For he on honey-dew hath fed,*
> *And drunk the milk of Paradise.*

He stared at the page, he stared out the window; he folded the paper into squares, and unfolded it again. He turned it over and wrote a rude limerick about a young man from Torquay. But, whatever techniques of concentration or distraction he tried, he could not write another line.

And, indeed, he never did find any way to move on. His poetic muse, previously a frequent visitor, came less often and more grudgingly from that day, and Coleridge eventually turned to criticism.

He never saw Joanna Siddeley again, and heard news of her only twice more. Gossip in the village told of her marriage to Viscount Hawker, a scant two months later: the bride, they said, had been radiant. And, out walking less than a year after that, Coleridge came upon a funeral procession making its way to the local churchyard. Recognising the squire and other local dignitaries, he asked a bystander the identity of the person being interred.

'Young Viscountess Hawker, sir. Died in childbirth, they say. Sad, isn't it, and her so young and full of life. But the babe is well, so some good has come of it all.' Coleridge said his thank-yous to the man, and ran for home, his purpose and his dignity forgotten. There was a triple dose of laudanum that night, and uneasy dreams for many nights thereafter.

Coleridge lived until 1834, as sharp as ever of mind but somehow broken and diminished in spirit. He eventually gave up his attempts to complete 'Kubla Khan', and published the fifty-four lines under his own name. He disguised their real inspiration with a cock-and-bull story that he had composed them in a dream and been interrupted in writing them down by the arrival of some man from Porlock on business. The story seemed desperately flimsy to Coleridge, but it was never doubted in his lifetime.

The boy whose birth was Joanna Siddeley's death lived to become a prosperous landowner and leading Tory; he resembled his mother in neither form nor temperament, save for brilliant green eyes that made him quite the beau of London. Of his views on poetry, or on the rights of women, no record survives.

THE SEEING

'HALT!' boomed an amplified voice, and soldiers sprang at them from the rocks. Rosie applied the brakes. Borren slipped his dark glasses on just as torchlight shone into the car.

A soldier came to the driver's side and demanded to know where they were going. 'Home,' said Rosie. 'Our house is on top of that mountain.'

'That house has been requisitioned as an observation post.'

'On whose order?' Borren demanded.

'And who might you be?'

'David Borren. My wife and I own the house.'

'My husband's blind,' Rosie added, as if that explained everything. 'Please let us go home.'

'Come with me,' said the soldier. 'I'll take you to Captain Lenihan.'

Leaving their car at the roadside, Rosie and David clambered into the soldier's jeep, with Rosie making a great play of assisting Borren across the uneven ground and inside. Ten minutes later, bounced and bruised, they were home.

'Thank you, Private,' said Captain Lenihan. 'That will be all.'

Lenihan was young and thin, with a burn mark on one cheek. He twisted his cap in his hands as he spoke.

'Under General Order 7184-A, civilian property may be requisitioned for war purposes. Every reasonable attempt is made to contact the property owner and arrange compensation or alternative accommodation. Unfortunately, we were unable to locate you.'

'We were in Santa Fe. I was scheduled for restorative surgery at the eye clinic, but the UCM got there first,' said Borren. 'Rosie's been driving non-stop since we got out. Why our house?'

'It's perfect for a forward observation post and fire-control base. You must have known what you were doing when you built this place — it's got the best view for miles around.' Lenihan stopped, glanced at Borren in confusion, and made an effort to regather his thoughts. 'Well, ah, we think the UCM will pass this way soon, and we need as much warning as possible.'

'Isn't that what your satellites are for?'

'Were for,' said Rosie. 'Remember?'

Borren recalled the brilliant flashes in the sky. At least he had been indoors, and looking away from the windows, at the time. 'How much time will you give us?'

'I can give you one hour to pack,' said Lenihan, 'then Sergeant Paterson will return you to your car. You've already been assigned a shelter in the city.'

Seventy minutes later, Rosie was still packing. Borren wished he could help, but Sergeant Paterson was hovering over them and pointing to her watch. 'Why don't you help her, then?' Borren demanded, and to his surprise Sergeant Paterson did.

Back at the checkpoint, the sergeant farewelled them with a volley of instructions for reaching the shelter.

It was nearly dawn when they reached the city. The sun was rolling up to the horizon, turning the eastern quarter of the sky a painful viridian, but it was still dark enough for Borren to read the map Captain Lenihan had sketched for them. They crawled their way through a crush of military vehicles and anxious civilians, refugees like themselves. Refugees, in America! They were almost out of gas by the time they found the right address.

There was nothing there but a door in the wall. They punched in the code, opened the door, and found stairs that led down to a warren of tunnels, some long-disused relic of the Cold War now pressed back into service. They followed the arrows to a dormitory with walls of steel. Lines of camp beds, most still unoccupied, stretched away into the distance.

Two weeks later, all the beds were filled.

Their life settled to a numbing monotony. They woke early, when the clamour of children and the threats of parents passed a critical threshold. One of them went to the shower line and the other to the food line, and with luck they would finish about the same time and be able to eat together. Then there was a briefing from Major Davis or Major Jimenez, who would tell them whether it was safe to go into the city today. It usually was, although twice Major Davis had been wrong, and they'd had to dive for cover as enemy planes roared overhead.

The city was no place for a blind man, real or pretend, and eventually Borren gave in to Rosie's pleas to stay underground while she went above. She would return with little trinkets or tidbits of extra food, but she was vague about where she got them. In his worst moments, Borren imagined her buying them with her body, screwing some soldier against the wall of a bombed-out alley.

If only he dared to read! But it was too risky. There were always people about, though they kept their distance from the grumpy old blind man on his bed. Sometimes he explored the corridors, tapping along with his cane until he came up against a locked door or a guard who gently turned him around.

A week into these explorations, he found a closed but unlocked door that led into a meeting room, and beyond it a kitchen. If he turned on the lights in the kitchen, opened the serving hatch, and sat at the far end of the darkened meeting room, the light was dim enough for him to read. That was a big improvement. He worked his way through the few books they had brought with them, and then asked Rosie to get him whatever she could; magazines, propaganda about the UCM, an old paperback with the spine torn off. And twice he brought her there and made love to her on the floor, stifling her moans with his hand in case they were discovered.

At night, Rosie slept soundly, but Borren tossed and turned, stray flashes of light stimulating his visual cortex. He had trained himself to be nocturnal, to sleep when the stars were no longer visible, and as the nights wore on he missed the seeing more and more. One night, there was a disturbance at the far end of the room: voices raised, a knife pulled. Guards rushed from everywhere to deal with it. Rosie opened one eye, looked around blearily, then settled back to sleep.

Borren got out of bed. Muttering something about the toilet, he tapped his way past the scuffle and through the exit door. Throwing off his caution, he ran down the corridor and past the empty guard station. He was free, and soon he was outside. He found a street where an enemy bomb had taken out the lights, climbed to the top of a pile of rubble, and removed his glasses.

The air was clear and calm, and the jewels of the Milky Way stood out in all their glory. He wanted to look, to marvel, and to forget. Off to the west was the Virgo Cluster, fifty million light years away, the new limit of his vision. Inwards he came, past galaxies, nebulae, stars, all in vivid colour. Then Mars: the polar caps, the volcanoes, the deep cut of the Valles Marineris. He knew there were still robots running around down there, sampling and building, reporting back; but was anyone still listening?

Inwards to the moon — but he could no longer look at the moon, for enough sunlight reflected off it to fill his new eyes with pain.

He had meant to spend no more than half an hour outside, then shuffle back, making some excuse to the corridor guard. It would not have been difficult to appear old, blind, and confused. But he forgot himself, and stayed out for almost two hours.

Rosie woke early, couldn't find Borren, and asked a guard for help. When Borren could not be found in the tunnels, she realised where he must have gone, but by then the search had acquired its own momentum. The soldier who found him saw him standing atop his pile of rubble, then the cane, lying unused at the base of the pile. Hearing his name called, Borren could not prevent himself from looking around.

For a while, they held him under guard in one of the abandoned meeting rooms. Rosie was allowed in to see him for a moment. Her stricken face told him all he needed to know, but he forced himself to smile at her. 'I'll be all right,' he said as she was taken away.

Then Major Jimenez came in, and the threats began.

—We kill spies.

—I'm not a spy.

—You're working for the UCM.

—I'm not working for the UCM.

They seemed disinclined to torture him, and he was disinclined to answer their questions. After a while, Major Jimenez went away. Major Davis came in, and shone a bright light in his face. That was agonising, but it didn't make him want to talk. Major Davis gave up after half an hour.

Two hours later, when the pain behind his eyes had almost gone away, Captain Lenihan and Sergeant Paterson arrived. Captain Lenihan brought food and coffee. Sergeant Paterson settled across the table and glared at him. This was so transparent that Borren almost laughed. Nevertheless, after half an hour of Lenihan's tentative kindness and Paterson's threats, he was ready to tell Lenihan everything. He blinked extravagantly, and saw them start as the silver membranes swept down and up again over the huge pupils of his eyes. 'Ask away,' he said.

'What happened to your eyes?' asked Lenihan.

'I replaced them with better ones.'

'Better in what way?'

'Better for seeing the heavens. These are stargazers' eyes, Captain Lenihan, the eyes I had installed in Santa Fe.'

'So you were never blind?'

'I was for the first week after the operation — it takes that long for the nerve endings to bed in. After that, given the situation, it seemed like the best cover. No sense getting murdered by a UCM zealot for violating some commandment or other.'

'How do they work?'

'My eyes are designed especially for stargazing. They've got a larger lens — well, you can see that — eight times standard transmittance, retinal images fifty times brighter

— everything I could wish for.'

'Any disadvantages?'

'My eyes bulge. Everything looks green in the daytime. I need to wear very dark glasses from dawn to dusk. It's nothing I can't handle.'

'Who paid for them?' asked Sergeant Paterson.

'The clinic. I'd kept in touch with Dr Summers from my NASA days. He offered me the chance to be a guinea pig. If things had worked out, my face would have started appearing in their ads in about three months' time.'

'Why you?'

'Dr Borren used to be an astronaut, Sergeant.' Lenihan glanced at his notes. 'The International Space Station, and then the second Mars mission, correct?'

'Yeah, then I was short-listed for the first mission to Europa. Do you know what happened to that?'

Lenihan shook his head.

'Six months before the launch date, with the ship almost completed in Earth orbit, Congress pulled the plug. Decided there were better things to do on Earth, like award their districts some more big defence contracts. The ship's still in orbit.'

'How do you know?'

'It passes over my house sometimes. If I could, I'd fly up there and take off for Jupiter tomorrow.'

'What about your wife?'

'I'd take her with me,' said Borren. 'Where is she?'

'She's fine,' said Lenihan. 'Now, Dr Borren, I have a proposition that may appeal to you. Would you like to return to your house and assist the war effort?'

'How?'

'Without our satellite information, and with our planes hidden away, we're effectively blind. What we need is someone to stand on that mountaintop and tell us where the UCM are and what they're up to.'

'The alternative is prison,' added Sergeant Paterson. 'They leave the lights on all night there.'

They set out later that day. Rosie wanted to go with Borren, but Lenihan refused, and threatened her with arrest if she persisted. She would have to stay in the shelter. Borren felt lost without her. He remembered the black days after his first wife left him, days when he took the gun from the desk drawer and played with it, putting it to his temple and pulling the trigger, only half sure there was no bullet in the chamber.

Rosie was a refugee from what was left of Havana. He met her one night in Gainesville, and since then she had stayed with him. He didn't know whether she loved him, and no longer greatly cared, so long as she was by his side. 'We'll be together soon,' he told her as he was led away.

They arrived back at the house in the late afternoon. It was in surprisingly good condition, although the bomb crater six metres from the back door did nothing for the resale value. 'Get some rest,' said Lenihan. 'You'll be on duty tonight.' Borren cleared military gear off the couch and lay down.

Three hours later, accompanied by an uncommunicative guard, he toiled up the path to the hilltop.

It was cold up there, and the next day the soldiers erected a little shelter for Borren and the guard. The fall stars were magnificent, but the guard would not let Borren stare at them for long.

Three nights later, Borren reported figures moving on a razorback ridge some twenty miles away. 'We'll deal with them,' said Lenihan. Borren waited. The figures clambered along the slope. He saw the brief flash of a torch, the glimmer of a cigarette. Near dawn, they dropped down the far side of the ridge, and the guard accompanied Borren back to the house.

'Well done,' Lenihan told him when he woke up late that afternoon. 'We hit them in the foothills. One survivor. They're talking to him now.'

'That's good, then. Are they going to come this way?'

'Sooner or later, yes.'

'Can we stop them?'

'I hope so,' said Lenihan. 'Why were you so keen to get your new eyes, Dr Borren?'

'I wanted to look at the stars. Just as I do now, when I get the chance. Look at the stars, and forget. I was getting a telescope built especially for me — ordinary ones are no use with these eyes, there's too much distortion and the field of view's too small — and then I would have been my own observatory. I had an observing programme all mapped out. But the telescope builder was also in Santa Fe, and he told me when we visited he wasn't planning to let the UCM scare him away. That kind of bravery can be terminal.'

'Are the stars so much better than the Earth?'

Borren smiled wearily. 'Ask yourself, Captain. What would you rather do, fight a war over the scraps of these United States or roam through the heavens?'

'I have my duty,' Lenihan told him. 'So do you.'

From that night on, though, the guard eased off Lenihan a little, and he was able to get some observing done.

Five nights later, the UCM made their move. There was no need for Borren to give an early warning: the waves of jets that roared overhead to bomb the city were warning enough. He couldn't look at the explosions, but none of them seemed to be nuclear. The cleansing fire of God evidently had its limits.

Rosie, he thought, I hope you got out; but he pictured her lying in the ruins, hands cupped across her belly.

The vanguard of the Army of God came into view around the base of the razorback ridge. It was huge. Lenihan had told him to watch out for the command units, whose members could be distinguished by the glittering crosses on their arms. Borren gave Lenihan their coordinates, and Lenihan decided which missile to fire at them.

It was quite something, to stand on this mountaintop and call down death on his enemies. One moment, he was watching the little figures march forward. The next, there was a flash, and when he could look back, there would be a crater, a cluster of broken bodies, and confusion in the enemy's ranks.

It couldn't last, of course. There were only so many

good vantage points, and the bomb crater showed that one of their pilots had already noticed this one. There was a flash at his back, a roar, and a shock that knocked him down. They had hit the house. He tried the radio a couple of times, but there was no answer. He had rather liked Lenihan, who had always been courteous to him.

There wasn't much to do after that. It was a still night, and the seeing was good. With his new pupils fully dilated, he drank in the photons that had travelled so far to reach him from the fields of glory overhead. Occasionally, smoke obscured the view, and he looked away for a time until it cleared. He was retracing the spiral arms of great Andromeda when he felt Rosie's hand touch his. He squeezed it gently. Together, they stared out across the great desert of stars.

AFTER THE WAR

When Takan neared the crest of the ridge, he turned and looked back. The sun was westering, and the air was filled with haze, through which he could make out the silver of the river. Somewhere below him, the army he had so recently deserted was being exterminated by the vengeful men of the west.

Well, let them die. They had staked everything on the invincibility of the Master, and lost. He had obeyed the Master, too: he had no choice. But, unlike his former comrades, he had considered what would happen if the Master failed.

It would have been simpler and safer to travel underground — the enemy was sure to have patrols venturing into these hills before long — but the catastrophe that had overtaken the Master had also destroyed many of the tunnels. His wounds stung in the harsh sunlight, but he pressed on.

He paused just below the ridgeline, reluctant to take the final few steps that would show him the plain beyond. When the Master's presence withdrew from his mind, and then vanished altogether, Takan had almost gone mad; many of his comrades had lost their minds completely, slaying themselves or each other.

He had hated the Master all his adult life, but the fact of him was inescapable, a dark and remorseless Father whose will was life and death. Now Takan was free, but he was also alone. He straightened as far as he was able, then strode to the top of the ridge.

The transformation was complete. What had this morning been a vast, mountain-encircled plain, crawling with the Master's armies and dominated by the Mountain and the Tower, was now a wasteland. The Tower had gone; in its place was a great pit half-filled with lava from the Mountain, which still belched fire and choking ash. On the plain, tiny figures ran hither and yon, despairing.

The sight confirmed what he already knew. The Master was dead. There lay in ruins the force that had dominated his life, had shaped it from the moment he awoke, blind and mewling, in the foetid darkness of the spawning-pool. Whatever hopes or desires he once had for himself had been swept away by the iron will of the Master, a will that drove the orcs to fight each other, to quarrel with their neighbours, to slay all who would not submit.

Some of his fellows had been fanatical followers of the Master, but most of the orcs had simply looked upon

Him as a force of nature, to be endured and obeyed. They would whisper together, when they thought themselves safe from his spies, of what they would do after the War: set up somewhere by themselves, with no men or devils to tell them what to do, and slaves and food always close at hand. They would whisper, and hope, but they would never plan.

Now he was scrambling down the hillside towards the smoking plain, using his long arms for balance. He would need to make his move at night, and soon, before the patrols of the enemy dared to venture this far. But it would not be easy.

He found the entranceway he was seeking and ducked inside. This tunnel was broader than those on the other side, and though rubble had fallen in places, it was never entirely blocked. He made his way into the heart of the rock by the dim light of torches set in the wall that were now burning down, untended by the slaves who had spent their lives in keeping these tunnels lighted. He should have been challenged by guards long ago, but they had fled like all the rest.

Here it was, the path to the forbidden place. By entering it, he would break one of the most fundamental taboos of his people. Takan hesitated, then drove himself on. Was he a slave, to be turned aside by custom or instinct?

The great space he entered was not lit. There was movement in the darkness, and a voice.

'It is not your time. Why are you here?'

'The Master is dead.'

'I know. Where are the slaves?'

'Fled or died.'

'Then Death comes for us all.'

'That is why I have come to you, Mother. Our enemies have triumphed. Soon they will enter these hills. Not all of them are blind in the darkness. They will find you.'

'I cannot leave this place. Go now.'

'I wish to, Mother. I wish to find new lands where our people may thrive. But there is no point in making such a journey without a female.'

'There are no females here. Has the Master not said that such Mysteries are sacred?'

'Great Mother, the Master is dead. His commands no longer bind us. He made such laws that we should not slip from his grasp. Now he is dead, and most of us with him. I wish to live. Although it is not my time, that time will come, and then, with a female, I can begin the task of rebuilding the People.'

'There are no females. How can there be? I am the Mother here.'

'That is so, but once I was told of the change that can come upon the hatchlings when a Mother dies . . .'

He waited nervously in the dark and the silence. When she spoke again, her voice was softer.

'You have profaned the Mysteries. For that, the penalty has long been death. Yet I see that there is some cause for hope in what has happened, and that many laws must now be set aside. I shall think on this. I am hungry. Bring me food.'

Takan was not accustomed to being commanded like a slave, and preparing a meal was an ignoble task for a warrior. But the stores were still full of food, brought there by the labour of many slaves from the wide lands he hoped to reach. He made a makeshift sled from sacks, piled it high with meat and black bread, and towed it back to the Mother's pool.

'Bring light,' she ordered.

He took a torch from the wall, and saw his mother for the first time. He had been blind when taken from the pool; she had been old even then. Now she squatted in water filled with drifting eggs and small, darting creatures. She was huge, black, and bent, one side of her body twisted towards the water which rose to her armoured belly. She raised her great head and bared her teeth.

'The meat. Bring it to me.'

He stepped into the pool, then stopped, confused, as he felt small teeth close on his leg.

'They're biting you, are they? They bite me also, but their teeth are too small to harm me. They live off the eggs, and each other. When I die, they'll live off me for a time, and grow strong, and a few will become females. It won't be long now.'

'But, Mother, the Mysteries—'

'If you are to succeed in preserving our people, you must learn all these Mysteries, and soon. Can you block the passage to the outside?'

'No. Only another earthquake could do that.'

'Let us hope it does. I felt the great one as the Master

fell. Come on, bring me the food . . . I can't move that arm, you fool. Here, put it in my mouth.'

Massive jaws, twice the size of his own, sheared through the meat he gave her. He waited in the water.

'You wish to leave me,' she said, when she had sated her hunger. 'Who will feed me then?'

'There is still much food in the stores, Great Mother.'

'But no one to bring it to me, and I can no longer leave this pool.'

'If I find any slaves or immature males, I will direct them here.'

'You would stay here yourself and feed me, if I ordered it. My will is still stronger, stripling.'

He felt the force of that will in his mind, where previously the will of the Master had drowned out lesser powers.

'Yes, you could,' he replied. 'But it is likely that the enemy will find this place, and then we will die. Are there other Mothers in these hills?'

'None that I know of.'

'Then do you want those maggots from the north, skulking in their mountains until the stone-eaters hunt them down, to be the last of our kind?'

'No, I do not. Can you see the far side of the pool?' She gestured awkwardly with her one free arm. 'There lie those of my brood who have outgrown the swimming stage but are not yet ready for the land. They lie as if dead while changes go on within them, and need neither food nor care. I can will them to remain in this state until roused.

Once their bodies have bowed to my will, you can take them with you. Put them in a sack and sling it over your shoulder.'

'How will I rouse them when the time is right?'

'Submerge their heads in water. Their bodies will take this as a sign that the breeding-pool is flooding, and they will wake to make their way to dry land.'

'When may I take them?'

'In a day's time. Go now, and await my command.'

So Takan waited, prowling the tunnels, thinking of the wide lands to the south and east. It was hot there, he had learned from the chatter of the slaves, and the sun shone fiercely, but the nights were cool and the waters ran pure in the shadow of the mountains. There he would build his empire.

The command from the Mother came as he was returning from another restless patrol of the outer halls: no enemy had tried to enter, but no friend either. He covered the network of twisting tunnels at a run.

'Where are they?'

The Mother pointed with her free arm. On the far edge of the pool, forms half-newt, half-orc lay with their heads above the water. Each was about a foot long, and the scaly, fish-like skin was beginning to give way to the hide of the mature orc. He picked them up and carried them, stacked like firewood.

'Go on. Put them in the bag. They won't notice.'

She watched as he followed her instructions.

'Now give me more of the meat, then go.'

He did as he was bidden. Before departing with his burden, he turned for a final look at the Mother. Her head was bowed, her left side dragging in the water.

'Mother . . .'

Go, came the command in his head. He turned and left her there.

Before he left the caverns, he had topped the sack up with food and selected a knife to go with his sword. Once deep night had fallen, he set out. He was too heavily laden to scramble over the shifting rock of the hillside, and the network of tunnels was broken for ever. He would have to take his chances on the plain.

The fires of the Mountain had burned lower, although smoke still coiled from its summit, but smaller fires were dotted about the plain. Some might be still-glowing flows of lava, but he feared that many were campfires. Friend or foe, they would have to be avoided.

He had travelled an hour or more, skirting the jumbled flanks of the mountains, when he felt a touch on his mind. *Help*.

The call didn't seem to be directed at him. It was the mind of some creature in mortal terror reaching out to anyone who might aid it. He supposed, since he had felt it, that it must be another orc. Now that the Master had gone, could every orc communicate in this way? Had there been a time before the Master when they all had done so?

No matter. These things, and this pitiful creature demanding his aid, were not his concern. The future of his race was. He walked a few more paces, and the call came again, more clearly. It was ahead of him, then. He realised that he could not pass it by.

Fifty more paces, and he could see the light of a campfire. It was burning at the mouth of a gully — a poor thing, fuelled by scraps of dead wood. The orc lying next to the fire moved slightly, and the call came again. Takan crept forwards.

It was a tribute to the strength of the breed that the orc was still alive. One of his arms had been severed, and there were deep cuts in his legs, chest, and belly. When he opened his mouth, it was apparent that his tongue had been cut out. Takan looked at the orc for a moment — not as an ally, not as a rival, but as a brother. Then he raised his sword and cut off his brother's ravaged head.

He was still off balance from the stroke when he heard the man behind him. He dodged, and the man's blow went wide. There were two of them, tall men and grim, trying to trap him against the rock wall behind the fire. He could abandon his burden and scramble to safety up the gully — but he would not abandon his burden.

'This one fancies himself a fighter, Egbar,' one of the men said. They were both keeping out of range of Takan's sword, but with their greater reach they were pressing him backwards. There was nothing for it. He dropped the sack, seized the knife from his belt, and hurled it at Egbar, jumping backwards as the other man's sword swept down. Takan's knife took Egbar in the throat. The other man's sword, missing Takan, plunged down through the sack. A dark fluid began to seep out onto the ground.

In the moment it took the man to retrieve his sword, Takan was upon him. He struck savagely, feverishly, dreading what he would find when he opened the sack. The man abandoned his sword and retreated to the fire. Picking up a burning brand, he thrust it at Takan. Every instinct screamed at him to retreat, but he advanced, ignoring the flame. The man retreated one step too far, tripped over the body of the orc they had tortured, and fell. He died before he could regain his feet.

Takan opened the sack in wild haste, throwing the food to the ground. He picked out one hatchling, then two. The third was transfixed by the sword. The gush of thick orc blood as he withdrew the sword told him that his sack would be lighter from now on. He hid the small body under rocks, repacked the sack, and moved on.

All that night, he feared pursuit, but none came. Anyone with the slightest knowledge of weapons and wounds would have been able to see that an orc had killed the two men, and that the dismembered orc that lay by them had been in no condition to do so. Perhaps there were those among the enemy who did not care to avenge the death of torturers.

When a lightening in the sky told of dawn to come, Takan headed for shelter in the hills. Before long he found a tunnel half-blocked by rubble. He scrambled over the rubble, rearranged it once inside to make a more imposing barrier, and made himself orc-comfortable on the hard stone.

It was time to sleep, but he could not sleep. The face of the dead orc tormented him. Why had he stopped to aid it? It was the voice, he decided, the voice in his head. Would even slaves and enemies now cry to him for mercy? He shuddered at the thought, and at last lay still.

He woke to fear and pain, his heart pounding. He willed himself to stillness. There was no sound of pursuit. What had woken him?

It was the Mother in her final agony. Across the miles, her mind called out to him, and he screamed too as the swords bit into her. He saw laughing faces, distorted with hate, and felt the breeding pool drain away around her. 'So this is how they spawn!' one of the men shouted. 'We've wiped them out for good now!' Then there was a final blow, and silence.

There was no more sleep for Takan that day. He sat in the dim light and mourned his mother and the last of the ways he had known. There was just him now, him and a sack.

Inside the sack, the two remaining hatchlings lay in a stillness even Takan could not match. On the surface, nothing about them had changed; but within, in the absence of the Mother, one was beginning the slow change into a female.

Shortly after dusk, Takan emerged from hiding and continued his journey. He clung to the skirts of the mountains at first, for the campfires still dotted the plain. By midnight, he had passed the last of them, and he struck out south-east across the plain. It was cold, and he was hungry, but he trudged onwards, bearing his burden of hope towards the distant peaks.

BEST PRACTICE

Cleve Cartmill Consulting was famous for the splendour of its office Christmas parties. Stories from the fabled 1980s of frolics on a chartered 737 and in a disused West Coast coalmine were the stuff of legend around the water-cooler.

Still, the late 1990s had not been without merit. The 1998 party was held in a fleet of hot-air balloons cruising above the Canterbury Plains, with grappling hooks supplied to aid social interaction. In 1999 it was black-water rafting and champagne at Waitomo.

Now it was Christmas 2000, and the team headed south again: from Wellington to Queenstown by chartered jet, from Queenstown to Wanaka in a fleet of light aircraft, and into the mountains by helicopter. They dropped out of the clouds to find a marquee waiting on a high plateau.

'Is that the best Cleve could do — a campsite?' sniffed

one of the Government Relations team. 'I thought we were in for something special this year.'

It had to be admitted that the view was spectacular. South of them, a saw-toothed mountain etched the sky. To either side, the land dropped away sharply into shadowed depths. To the north, a stream tinkled through rock and tussock.

Spectacular, and yet nothing that couldn't be seen in an advert for off-road vehicles or the more manly brands of beer. The procession of penguin-suited waiters trekking from supply tent to party marquee amid the bleak landscape was diverting, and the outfitting of the marquee itself left nothing to be desired, but among the guests the prevailing mood was one of faint disappointment.

Still, they were here to enjoy themselves, and the booze and the food were free. Christmas began to work its magic again. As the night wore on, cleavages grew more spectacular, tushes more enticing. Faces lined by age and fear regained the sheen of youth. Before long, couples could be found wherever nature and art conspired to afford privacy. Passion blossomed under the tables and amid the piles of empty serving dishes.

Some couples sought their bower outside. Night had fallen, however, and a thin and icy wind had risen to shrivel love and lust alike. The tents provided for the waiting staff (who had been flown in the day before) gained an immediate appeal. Purses and wallets were produced and bargains struck. At times during that night rows of waiters could be seen, shivering a discreet distance from their tents, cold but well rewarded.

As the night wore on, alcohol took its toll on all but the hardiest. The marquee was full of snores, belches, and farts. Cleve Cartmill stepped between the prone bodies and smiled. So far, it had all gone exactly to plan.

Preparations to dismantle the site began at 9am. Within half an hour, the bustle of orderly activity and the roar of incoming helicopters had woken even the most red-eyed. Before they departed, the waiters passed around water bottles and multivitamins, and from somewhere the miraculous smell of coffee was rising. But before there was time to savour it, the marquee and the Port-a-loos were helicoptered away.

The partygoers blinked in the bright morning sunlight. The view looked more impressive now, and even the most rugged off-road vehicle might hesitate to tackle these jagged peaks with their overburden of snow. It was cold, and they shivered, huddled together for warmth, and speculated about the tarpaulin-covered bundle that had been set down in place of the marquee.

As speculation turned to agitation, a shout: Cleve Cartmill and his black-clad HR team were approaching around a ridge to the east. They walked quickly, confident in the broken terrain. They halted. Cleve Cartmill held up his hand for silence.

'Thanks for coming, everyone,' he said. 'It's been a great party. My last party, because I've sold a controlling interest in the company to Nansen and Associates. They need to let quite a few of you go.

'We thought we'd design the selection process to reward initiative, so this is how it's going to work: we've set up the recruiting office for the restructured company in Haast. The first seventy of you to get there will keep your jobs.' He was having to shout now; a helicopter was descending behind him. 'Thanks for all your loyal service. Goodbye.' Before anyone could react, he was gone.

Even at the height of the party, HR had kept their distance, a taut-faced crew approached at one's peril. Now their leader stepped forward and raised her hand for silence. 'Mr Cartmill asked me to give you some additional information. We are within the boundaries of Mount Aspiring National Park. The plateau on which we're standing is located on the Main Divide at a height of fourteen hundred metres. It's called Rabbit Pass. To the east, the East Matukituki River drains into Lake Wanaka. To the west, the Waiatoto River drains into the Tasman Sea, south of Haast. This stream to the north is the headwaters of the south branch of the Wilkin, which drains into the Makarora River, which also drains into Lake Wanaka. Mr Cartmill wishes you to use best practice principles to find a solution to the current problem.'

'Does calling up a helicopter with a cellphone count?'

HR shook her head. 'This site has been carefully selected to be out of cellphone range. Has anyone brought a mountain radio or a GPS receiver?'

Silence.

'Good. Mr Cartmill has provided equipment for you: packs, boots, survival gear, rations and clothes. You'll find it's individually labelled. Please locate your gear and put it on.'

HR pulled back the tarpaulin to reveal the gear. It fitted well, though the new boots pinched. Now they knew why they'd been asked for so much biometric data a couple of months back. When they were dressed, HR called them back together.

'You will split into three groups to investigate the three options, then report back here in one hour. We will then decide a transparent, contestable process for resolving the problem. Now, please form into three groups.'

Cue aimless milling around in the best playground tradition.

'Very well, I'll count you off. East Team is one, West Team is two, North Team is three. One, two . . .'

East Team's route was blocked by the ridge around which Cleve Cartmill had appeared, so at first they had to go south, then make their way east towards the edge of the plateau. They walked to the edge. They stepped back. Very cautiously, they walked forward again, and looked down.

They were high above the head of the East Matukituki, and the first few hundred metres of the descent went almost straight down. The cliff was unbroken to their right and left. There was no way down that cliff without rope, a lot of rope. They had no rope.

'There's a ledge off to the left. Maybe things get easier that way?'

They trooped north-east along the narrow, bare ledge. After a kilometre or so, they found a gap in the cliff where broken blocks of grey stone sloped steeply down towards the valley far below.

'Looks like this is our only option. Guess we should get back and tell the others.'

'Get back and tell the others? You don't think those bastards are going to wait for us, do you? They're probably halfway to Haast already. You can go back if you like, but I'm getting down here as fast as my legs will carry me.' The speaker — one of those jut-jawed types from Corporate Affairs — set off. He had gone no more than two metres when the loose shale slipped beneath his feet. He sat down, hard, and slid almost to the edge of a small bluff before he found solid footing again. He rose to his feet and glared at them.

'Are you buggers going to stay there all day?'

They looked at each other, then, in ones and twos, started down to join him.

Meanwhile, West Team had made it to the western edge of the plateau and down into a gently-sloping basin with no trouble at all. 'This', one said, 'is going to be easy.'

It all started well for North Team, too, as they walked beside the chuckling stream. The ground sloped gently, the sun was shining, and they could hear the occasional piping of some alpine bird. There were flowers dotted here and there amid the rock and tussock. Their route was plain, and for good measure some helpful soul had marked it with tall orange poles. The poles continued right to the edge of the precipice that made this one of the most difficult tramping routes in New Zealand.

The drop mattered little to the fledgling south branch of the Wilkin River, which flowed merrily over the edge, fell straight down one hundred metres, bounced a couple of times, and resumed its wanderings on the flats below. But North Team would need ropes, parachutes, or wings to join it there.

They fanned out across the valley to look for a way down. At last, well to the west, they found what looked like a trail edging down a steep snowgrass slope above the cliff proper. Two of the party, veterans of the firm's indoor climbing wall, volunteered to investigate it.

'Hey, there's a ledge below the snowgrass! It's narrow and steep, but it's heading the right way. Who's coming with us?'

Not even the threat of redundancy would compel most of North Team to tackle the descent, but a few were willing to take the risk.

'Right, you lot have had your chance. We'll be halfway to Haast by the time you make up your minds.'

'You'd better hurry,' one of the refuseniks said. It was clouding over from the north. There was rain coming.

The sun was still shining on East Team, but the sweat was clammy on their brows. They had come down thirty metres from the ledge above, with many cries of panic as the loose rock shifted beneath their feet, but now they were stuck at the top of a ten-metre bluff, below which was a chute of icy snow.

'Why the hell didn't they give us any rope?'

'Too easy, maybe?'

'What the fuck, I'm going down.'

So saying, the hero from Corporate Affairs lowered himself over the edge, scrabbling for footholds. He found one and was searching for another when the rock he was using as a handhold gave way and he crashed to the ice below. By the time he had recovered from the shock of landing, he was sliding, with no way of slowing himself. The snow slope ended far below in a scatter of boulders. He struck them like a human luge, hitting the first boulder with his feet and the second with his head.

East Team watched for signs of life for a while, then began the climb back to safety. When they had almost reached their ledge, there was a shout of triumph.

'Hey, there's a way down here. See? And it comes out above the snow, on that gravel. What do you reckon?'

About half of them reckoned it was worth a go. The other half climbed back to the ledge, still shivering, and made their way back towards the campsite in the gathering gloom. As they got there, they could see the bedraggled remnants of West Team coming to join them. Everyone started talking at once.

'One report at a time, please!' said HR. 'West Team.'

'Shit, you've got to do something! Half our team are stuck in a gully, and Sally Wishart's broken her leg or something. We scrambled down into this basin and everything was fine till we got to the far side. There the stream shoots down through this gully filled with really big rocks. Some of us said that's way too dangerous, but

Sally kept saying she could see a way down, and a dozen of our team went with her. We can't see what's happened to them, but there was a rockslide, and Sally's in a lot of pain down there.'

'Is there an alternative way to reach the Waiatoto?'

'Some of us think there might be if you go way off to the left and up a bit.'

'Very well. East Team?'

But the report back from East Team was delayed, because the clouds opened and the rain fell in cold grey sheets. East and West straightened out the tarpaulin, put rocks around three edges, and crawled under it for shelter. The open side faced south, so the first they knew of North Team's return was the sound of their stumbling feet.

'Two of us went over the edge! And half the rest are stuck on a ledge, and water is starting to flow down it.'

'Over the edge? How far?'

'Maybe sixty metres.'

Rain and overconfidence are never a good mixture in the mountains. The two indoor climbing experts had found a way down from the snowgrass onto a succession of mossy ledges, but rain-slicked rock and moss make for poor footing. A false step, a grab at the other for support, and two bodies were lying on the snowgrass fan at the base of the cliff. Those following them had tried to turn back, but it was too dangerous to move. The watchers from above had left a couple of hardy souls on the lip of the cliff and come back for help.

'Can't you call in a helicopter or something?'

HR nodded. 'It's about time.' They produced a mountain radio and set up the aerial. The clouds had lifted by the time the helicopters came. One headed for North Team's ledge. The other dropped directly in front of the campsite, and Cleve Cartmill stepped out. 'Welcome aboard, people,' he said.

By the time the other helicopter came to pick up the two shattered corpses from the snowgrass below them, the sun had started to shine again on the shivering, ledge-bound remnant of North Team. The group had split in two, half edging uphill to safety, half downhill to glory. The ascending half made their way back to the campsite and a waiting helicopter, while the descending half were left to fend for themselves. The rest of their descent was accomplished in tiny steps and terse whispers, but once they were on the flats below the cliff, it was comparatively easy to make their way down the south branch of the Wilkin to its junction with the north branch, where they found a hut to stay for the night.

The next morning, it was full speed ahead down the Wilkin to the Makarora. Standing on the western bank of the Makarora, they could see cars on the Haast Highway across the river. That was when someone discovered they were back in cellphone range, and within half an hour the first jetboat had arrived to take them across the Makarora's unfordable depths. Once the first boatload reached the eastern shore, the race to Haast was on in earnest. By dawn the next day, all those who had survived the descent had dragged their weary bodies into the township.

It was two hours after that before the first East Team member reached Haast. Having made it off the treacherous shale with no further casualties, they had pressed on down the East Matukituki Valley until they reached the fearsome Bledisloe Gorge. It took a lot of time, and two near-drownings, to conclude that it wasn't a good idea to tackle it by heading straight downriver. It took longer still to find that the only safe route lay high above them to the left. By the time they got past the gorge, most of them were revising résumés in their heads as they trudged the weary miles to Cameron Flat and the start of the road.

West Team was later still. After Sally Wishart had been helicoptered to safety, the remaining Westies had held a team meeting, as frank as it was open. Then they clambered back to the gently sloping basin, paid better attention to their surroundings, and found a difficult but safe way down. Of course, that still left them in the upper reaches of the Waiatoto River, with its sudden floods, its water milky with rock flour, its gorges, and its dangerous crossings. They were a long way from their destination.

But at last, every surviving employee of Cleve Cartmill Consulting made it out of the mountains. All those who stumbled and struggled to Haast after the harrowing descent from Rabbit Pass were met at the temporary Nansen and Associates office by Hannelore Nansen, given a mug of coffee and a pat on the back, and told to go right on through to HR, don't bother about washing. Sudha from HR was there, and she stood behind her desk and handed them each a letter of termination and their tickets back to Wellington. 'Contact Security to retrieve your personal effects from the office,' she said. 'Your redundancy cheque is enclosed. Good luck!'

The seventy who passed the test — all those who had given up on the three hazardous descents, plus the HR team — were whisked back to Head Office in Wellington to find the furniture changed, the walls repainted, and the Nansen and Associates logo everywhere. Soon they were back on the job, greenwashing the image of the country's worst polluters and setting up artificial grassroots groups to oppose the real ones. The latest was Citizens for Wise Use of National Parks, a front for the mining industry. Many survivors of the selection exercise were more than happy to sign up for that one.

The selection exercise had cost three lives, and there was some muttering in official circles; but Nansen and Associates knew how to spread the corporate goodwill around, and before long it was concluded that an enquiry would be an unjustified drain on the public purse. Death by misadventure was common enough in the mountains.

The 2001 Nansen and Associates Christmas function was held in the office. After far too many whiskies, some idiots decided to traverse the outside of the building, from balcony to balcony. A few people popped their heads out the window to watch, but it was cold out there, and the party was humming indoors. A little later, there was a scream, then another. The party fell silent for a moment.

'Wanted: Web Developers. Must have no head for heights,' someone said. And even HR laughed at that.

ROBINSON IN LOVE

Lisa gave Robinson a knife, a bowl, a chopping board, and three tomatoes. Later, she gave him lettuce, cucumber, and carrots. By the time he'd run out of ingredients, he had made a salad, and Lisa had cleared the table, split bread rolls, and set out slices of Camembert and little pottles of dips and spreads. Robinson would have settled for Marmite.

He wasn't sure where to sit. There was the table, overflowing with food, with three wooden chairs around it, and off in the distance a couple of armchairs and a sofa. Would sitting on the wooden chairs be too formal, would heading straight for the sofa be too familiar? He waited for her lead.

'You okay?'

'Oh yes, fine, fine. That's a great view you have there.' Squint and you could see a corner of the harbour gleaming in the sun.

'It's better from the deck. Let's go outside.'

They put their plates on a small white table shaded by a sun umbrella. Surely that wouldn't stay up for long in Wellington's winds. She must have erected it especially for his visit — a good sign, Robinson decided.

She went inside to get drinks, and he watched her. What was she wearing? Robinson forced himself to concentrate: he wasn't good on such details, but he knew they were important. A patterned blouse — was it silk, or would that be too thin for the conditions? But maybe silk was warmer than it looked. Red trousers. The same sort of outfit she had on yesterday, with some changes to the actual clothes.

She was coming outside again. Should he look debonair? He decided that debonair was not in his range. Be yourself, young Kevin, that's all you can ever be.

She joined him at the railing, and as they talked of the view, he wanted only to slip his hand in hers, put his arm around her, nuzzle her neck with his lips.

A fly was buzzing at the food. She shooed it away, and they sat down.

Some of his nerves had eased, and he was hungry. This was good, to sit in the sunlight, eating summer food, drinking wine with a beautiful woman. He, Kevin Robinson, thirty-two years old, unlovable and unloved, was lunching with a beautiful woman. Who owned her own home. It was wooden, and needed painting. The back garden was small, falling away on one side; broken trellis-work climbed up a rusty iron fence. He would take it down, pile rocks against the fence, plant—

She had asked him a question. Sorry, said Robinson, ask me again.

'Do you realise we've met before?'

Oh hell. How to answer this? 'No' was truthful. 'Yes' would sound better, but carried risks of its own.

'No. When?'

'At the conference in '93. Do you remember that party in Don Archer's room?'

'Where the hotel management threatened to evict everyone if we didn't keep the noise down?'

'So Don moved the party to the lift?'

Robinson smiled. He remembered, all right. He had had a thing for Maria Osbourne then, and had spent most of the night trailing disconsolately after her from room to room and party to party. About midnight, she had disappeared with her arms around that woman from the Scripps Institute. After ten minutes standing on a balcony looking at the welcoming pavement below, he had thought to hell with it and headed straight for Party Central, which was bound to be Don Archer's room. Twenty minutes of that and he was down in the lobby, talking with a few other refugees from the noise. There was Irihapeta Purvis, Dave Sims, and this other woman . . .

'That was you in the lobby!'

'That's right, sitting on the arm of Dave Sims' chair. I was tired, but you looked half-dead. I couldn't work out if you were drunk or just depressed.'

'What sort of fool did I make of myself?'

'A quiet one. I thought, he's kind of cute, in a woebegone way.'

'You looked cute too, but I thought, you know, Dave Sims . . .'

'Oh, no. Dave and I have known each other for ages. Did you know he got married last year?'

'Someone I know?'

'No, a lawyer. Anyway, you sat there for a while, and then you said, "I have been on my feet for eighteen hours and it's too loud even here," and staggered away.'

'I must have been sozzled. I don't remember much about the next day. But why the hell didn't I recognise you this year? You look different somehow . . .'

'I was a redhead then.'

'Of course. Well, it makes a big difference. You look so good.'

'Thank you.'

There was something in her expression — had he offended her? What the hell. Press on regardless.

They ate. The wind rose, so they went inside. He sat on the sofa with his plate balanced on his knee and the wineglass on the speaker. She sat opposite, legs tucked beneath her. Probably she did yoga or something like that.

They talked about this year's conference. He came every year; this was her first since '93. Neither was an academic in the strict sense: she was a mapmaker, he a map curator. They would make a good couple, thought Robinson: yes, a good couple, together, in a house like this, waking up in the morning, eating breakfast, cleaning their teeth, going to work, coming home. They would have lunch together when the weather was nice, sitting by the waterfront, looking at the waves.

Lucky, so lucky to have met again yesterday. The conference proper was over, and most of the out-of-towners were waiting for transport in the hotel lobby. Robinson was there too, but he had decided to stay an extra night and catch a cheap flight back on the Tuesday. He was considering his options for the rest of the day:

1. Stay in the hotel and attend the AGM of the New Zealand Mapmakers' Circle, thus spending the afternoon debating constitutional amendments.
2. Head out the door and go somewhere, anywhere: to the movies, or the beach, or walking in the hills.

A hip came by. It had a nametag on it. 'Oh, you're Lisa Bryant!' Looking up at her, catching his breath.

'That's right. And this means?'

That took some explanation: how Ben Drummond had been talking about her before the conference, how Ben thought she would be interested in the exhibition Robinson was curating, how Robinson ought to get in touch with her. 'I hear she likes geeks like you, Robbo,' Ben Drummond had said, chucking him under the chin. That had put Robinson off, and he had made no effort to find her.

Lisa and Robbo talked in the lobby for ten minutes or so. Robinson told her about his exhibition, 'Continuity and Change'. The punters would enter beneath an archway of ice and be taken through a history of Antarctica in maps, from the early efforts of Bellingshausen and Palmer right through to the present day. Continuity, because the attitudes of those explorers — the awe and the fear — were still mirrored today; change, because the continent itself was changing. Then he saw Lisa looking at her watch. He paused.

'I'm going to the dining room for lunch,' said Lisa. 'Do you want to join me?'

Robinson watched his answer slide from his mouth, each word glistening wetly on its way to her ears.

'I can't, sorry. I've got to go to the AGM.'

'Oh,' she said. He fancied she looked disappointed. 'See you round, then,' she said, and headed off to the dining room.

An inky wave of gloom rolled over Robinson, pressing him deep into his chair. He stared up through it at the dim lights, the ceiling, the palm fronds waving like seaweed. He had caught her, and then he had tossed her back.

Kevin, he told himself, it's now or never. He got up, wiped his eyes, and walked. Through the doors, up the stairs, turn left. She was sitting with her back to him, waiting for her order to arrive. He tapped her shoulder and said look, I really do have to go to this AGM, but I don't leave town till tomorrow afternoon. Maybe we could do something tonight? Or tomorrow?

Lisa smiled, guardedly, and said, I'm busy tonight (and oh, the pang in his heart at those words) but how about lunch tomorrow, then she could run him out to the airport afterwards?

And so she had picked him up from the hotel today, taken him with her to the supermarket to buy the lunch things — unexpected and nerve-wracking, this, as Robinson tried to cope with twenty types of exotic cheeses and a profusion of specialty breads — and now here they were.

'Do you like music, Kevin?' she asked.

'Well, I like some music . . .'

'What sort of music?'

'Oh, I guess — well, I don't like country at all, and I've never been very keen on folk, or rap, or disco . . . Eighties stuff, mainly, and a few newer bands — Massive Attack, Radiohead.'

'How about jazz?'

'Never really listened to it. Do you?'

'When I feel like it.'

Robinson watched her stretch to the CD rack, bend to the player, fold gracefully back into her chair. It was Billie Holiday. He had noticed that women liked Billie Holiday — all that melancholy, all that washed-out regret. It wasn't really his cup of tea.

'Do you like to dance?'

Oh no, thought Robinson. Please, not that. Last night, he had run through a range of possible disasters, but he had never thought it would come to this. In Standard Three, the teacher, Mr Willis, had made them do folk dancing. Mr Willis concealed an elderly record-player somewhere about his person and would, with the aid of a series of frayed extension cords, set it up in the playground. He would then produce one of a series of records by Alex Lindsay and His Orchestra, put it on, and order the children to line up in pairs and do the strathspey, or the springle-ring, or whatever other bizarre form of torture appealed to him that day. Mr Willis would (for those were innocent times) take the hand of some mortified girl and lead her through the required steps while the other children watched silently. Then he would remove the needle, return the tone arm to the beginning of the record, and watch as the children shuffled around, with a hey-nonny-no and a tirra-li-li and a bow for Good Queen Bessie. If they performed below Mr Willis's expectations, they would still be out there dancing when playtime came around. The taunts of the younger children rang in Robinson's ears every time 'dance' was mentioned. The most he was prepared to do was flail away, energetic but uncoordinated, the archetypal white boy, when the floor was already packed and no one was watching. But this? Dance to Billie Holiday? With a woman?

'Well,' said Robinson, aware that he was saying 'well' a lot, 'not really . . .'

'There's nobody watching.'

'You'll be watching.'

'No I won't. I'll be dancing, and I'm shorter than you.'

He suffered himself to be raised up from the sofa and drawn into her arms. There was some low-key debate about who should lead, but in the end they kicked off their shoes and compromised. Billie Holiday was singing about reaching for the moon. 'You don't have to leave your hands on my shoulders,' Lisa murmured. He slid one hand down her back, as his mother had once tried to teach him.

After a minute or so, Robinson relaxed enough to regain some body awareness. There were conflicting signals. Lisa's hair was tickling his nose; he turned his head away slightly and tried not to sneeze. Her breasts were pressing against his chest, which was pleasant. And there was his erection, which she must be able to detect. Surely this would not surprise her. It was perfectly natural, after all.

They danced for about ten minutes, silent but for an occasional whispered apology, then she slipped from his arms and smiled at him.

'I enjoyed that,' said Robinson.

'Mmmm. I won't be long.'

She headed off to the bathroom. Robinson's thought followed her. She was taking a while in there. Was she putting in a contraceptive? Dutch cap, pessary; there was a whole menagerie of them. Robinson always carried a couple of condoms in his wallet, just in case, but they were probably well past their use-by date by now. Anyway, he mustn't make assumptions. He knew he should sit still and relax, but he couldn't. He was clearing away the lunch things when she returned. She joined him, smiled at him, opened her mouth —

'Tell me more about that exhibition of yours.'

Disappointed, relieved, Robinson marshalled his

thoughts. 'Well, we didn't think a bunch of maps would be enough to draw in the punters, so we've got a ride as well. It's based on the break-up of the North Larsen Ice Shelf back in '95. The Animation Research people did it for us — you know, the America's Cup people?'

'That must have cost you. How does a provincial museum find that sort of money?'

'Grants. There's still money in Dunedin if you know where to look. Anyway, they've done it from the perspective of someone standing on an ice floe a kilometre or so away from the edge of the shelf. You see these huge icebergs crashing down and floating towards you, towering over you, sliding right past your nose. They've built in the noise, the cold, the whole bit. Left me shaking the first time I tried it, and I knew what to expect. We're trying to flog it off to the Antarctic Centre in Christchurch once the exhibition closes.'

'Sounds a lot more exciting than anything I get to do.'

'But it's you who's in the right line of work. Know why?'

'Let me guess. Global warming, so sea levels will keep rising, so maps will keep needing to be redrawn.'

'Six metres if the West Antarctic Ice Sheet goes. And, you know, it might. They're very concerned about basal melting of the Pine Island Glacier at the moment, and . . .' She was looking at him quizzically. 'What?'

'Just thinking what a strange man you are. We've had lunch, we've danced a little, you've got a plane to catch and what are you doing? Telling me about basal melting.'

'Well, you asked about work . . .'

'I'm a little nervous, too.'

'I'm sorry about the dancing: it was like being back at school—'

'The dancing was fine. Let's go back in the lounge, huh?'

He followed her to the sofa. They sat side by side.

'Was I really so boring?'

'No, not boring. One day, we'll clear our diaries, and you can tell me all about the West Antarctic Ice Sheet and how the Pine Island Glacier holds it in place, and how the Larsen B Ice Shelf broke up in a few weeks in 2002, and how people think the East Antarctic Ice Sheet is safe, but really it isn't, and if that goes we'll all be swimming to work. Agreed?'

Robinson sagged like a deflated balloon, and she bent over and kissed him on the mouth, her lips warm and damp against his, her tongue chasing his into its lair. It was hard to breathe. She pushed him back against the cushions and straddled him, so that he was straining upwards into her through four layers of clothing. When he put his hands to her breasts, she kissed him all the harder. He rubbed her nipples through the cloth, thinking to hell with the plane, thinking oh please please. He was tugging down her trousers when she took her tongue out of his mouth, pulled away, stood up. Face pink, breath ragged, she smiled.

'Time to go, Kevin.'

'Time to go?'

'Time to go. Or you'll miss your flight.'

'But—'

Five minutes later, he was in the car. Ten minutes after that, they were at the airport. He got in the queue while she brought the luggage on a trolley. Nearly five minutes till the boarding call. Could they find somewhere — the toilets, a baggage trolley, the stairs? His balls ached. She was talking: something about her holidays, something about writing.

'I'll write tonight,' said Robinson, and he meant it. Pages and pages, as soon as he got home and turned on the computer. He would put on some music, type till his wrists ached and post it tomorrow. (Maybe he'd email it as well, to be on the safe side.)

Would she write back? That was the question.

More talk. Then his plane was called, and he stood to go. She stood with him, kissed him, rubbed her hand gently up his leg and across his groin, so that he approached the boarding counter holding his bag in front of him for modesty. They kissed again. 'I love you,' he said as he left her.

She smiled. 'Write,' she said.

He backed down the air bridge waving, swapped to a window seat, carried on waving like a maniac until the plane was airborne. He had seen her there, on the viewing platform, maybe. Magazine, snack, this is your captain speaking, we're flying at an altitude of twenty-five thousand feet into a slight south-westerly, those sitting on the right will get a good view of the Clarence River and the Seaward Kaikouras, we should arrive in Christchurch a little after . . . He listened with half an ear, playing with his biscuit wrapper, smiling out the window at the blue Antarctic sea.

GOING UNDER

Martin Fisher had never learned to swim. He had been a tall, scrawny boy, and always told enquirers that he'd never had enough blubber or trapped air to float. There was no physiological basis for this claim, and in truth he remembered school swimming lessons as painful occasions. He was scared of large groups of noisy children, always had been, still was. They splashed and yelled relentlessly. He hugged his thin, cold body and shrank back from the pool. The teachers enjoyed swimming time no more than he did, and had little sympathy for shirkers, so in the end he would climb down the slippery ladder into the pool and cling to the rail, kicking his legs reluctantly, until they were all called back to the changing rooms, where further humiliation waited to pounce.

He grew from scrawny boy through big-boned adolescent to a solid young man whose waistline softly expanded as the years slid by. He enjoyed trips to the beach: throwing frisbees, soaking up the sun and even splashing in the cold Dunedin surf. After a good half-hour's splashing, he'd resolve to take those Adult Learn-To-Swim classes he'd been promising himself for years. But there was the thesis to finish and the world to save, and he never quite found the time.

Early in the final year of his thesis, before he heard back from the Institute for Climatic Change in Boston, he travelled with some friends to Smaills Beach to soak up the sun and take advantage of the water. Martin lay in a sandy hollow at the top of the beach, just inside the sandhills, for a while, talking with his new flatmate Chris. But the sea looked inviting, and he dragged himself to his feet and down to the water's edge. He dipped his toe in, and decided the water was getting warmer by the year. Of course, seasonal fluctuations were always— Stop thinking, Martin, he told himself, and get in there! He advanced to calf-deep, to thigh- and hip-deep (having postponed the inevitable shock when the water first touched his balls); he savoured the ebb and surge of the streaming water.

When the troughs of the swells were reaching his chest and the crests were lifting the hair from his neck as he turned to let them pass, he decided that he'd come far enough, and started back. Turning, he was caught off balance by a wave approaching the beach on an angle, warped by the longshore current. It washed him off the sandy hummock on which he had been standing and deposited him on the floor of a pit almost a metre deeper.

The water climbed above his shoulders and his head. Only his frantically waving arm broke the surface.

He had a couple of minutes to live. He leapt upwards; his head breached the surface, and he took a mouthful of foam and air. No one was nearby. He yelled, but the water swallowed his cry and surged into his lungs. Another jump, a half-breath, then a wave broke over his head and he was submerged again. A third jump; this time, he barely broke the surface before falling back.

Martin was well under this time, and his legs were tiring. He tried to make the air in his lungs last and even had time to look about him. Despite his panic, he noticed the colour of the light — Steinlager green — and the undulations of the sea floor. I'm going to die here, he thought. Water and bubbles flashed before his eyes. He could feel himself fading. Well, one last jump for old times' sake . . .

The current was an impartial thing. It had prowled that shore for ages, carving out headlands at the northern end of each beach, working with the waves to scour the bottom. It had swept him out of his depth, and with his life some thirty seconds from its end, as he tried one last jump for air, it swept him out of the pit and back onto higher ground. His head rose above water; he breathed raggedly, coughed up a specimen of the brine that had nearly claimed him, and staggered towards the shore. Through good luck or instinct, he avoided dropping down into another pit. Chris was running towards him. His other flatmates followed. Soon Martin was enfolded in comfort, succour, concern.

He spent the next hour coughing up water and feeling wretched. By the time they passed the beachside dairy on the way home, though, he was feeling up to an ice cream.

Two weeks later, he returned home from another hard day in his tiny carrel in the university library to find a letter from Boston. If you can finish your thesis in time, it said, we want you over here. For the next three months, Martin was no more to his flatmates than a pale shadow that flitted through the door at midnight and left by eight the next morning. Sometimes, they discovered, he'd get up a half-hour earlier and perform an imitation of housework before he went. A week before his departure, thesis complete, he apologised to his flatmates by throwing a big party, and staying around to clean up afterwards.

Then the well-lit mills of American academia claimed him as their own. Over the next twenty years he had churned out papers, delivered lectures, secured tenure, seen the inside of a hundred conference centres and a hundred hotel rooms. At one such conference, 'Littoral Zone Submergence: First Results of the ICC Study', he had been invited to the bed of a geomorphologist from MIT. Such liaisons were traditional at scientific conferences, but this one led to an invitation to dinner back in Boston, and then to a relationship that lasted long enough for Martin to see Ana complete her PhD and secure a junior lectureship — in Wyoming.

For the first time, his dedication to his career wavered. He could move to Wyoming; the university there would find a place for him, and he could continue, after a fashion, with his work. But the ICC was where it was at, one of the three major centres of climate change studies, consulted by the presidents of countries and corporations, a place where you might shape the future of the world. In the end, Ana went to Wyoming, and Martin traded favours to get himself on the ICC's next Antarctic team.

Antarctica was swarming with scientists, tourists, and journalists doing solemn pieces to camera. Moves to restrict the number of people on the continent at any one time were afoot, and though Martin supported such restrictions, he was delighted to have the chance to pre-empt them. Walking along the Dry Valleys — imagining them repopulated with ferns, conifers, and thunder-footed lizards — was a fine antidote to nostalgia and regret. More ominous, though, was a visit to the edge of the West Antarctic Ice Sheet to watch the icebergs calving, icebergs that would melt and add their water to the slowly swelling seas.

Martin and Ana still saw each other at conferences. They made a point of going out for dinner when they got the chance. Sometimes, for old times' sake, they made love.

And now here he was, Professor Martin Fisher, distinguished researcher, noted expatriate, back in New Zealand to chide the bureaucrats and condescend to the media. Here he was, walking down Centre Road to Smaills Beach.

Things were certainly different from twenty years

earlier. There were oranges growing here now, despite the wispy southerly that retained traces of its Antarctic origin. He plucked one from an overhanging branch and sampled it as he went along. The farmers of Otago weren't complaining about climate change, unless their land was so low-lying it had been reclaimed by the sea: the province had become the fruit-basket of the country, and Central Otago kiwifruit a worldwide delicacy. The air of self-satisfaction had been palpable from the moment he stepped off the plane. On hearing he'd been away so long, people's standard response was, 'You should see the weather forecasts now!' Dunedin was still colder than points north, but with much of the North Island now plagued by cyclones and the Ross River virus, that was a point in its favour.

Well, he thought, they won't be smiling for long. He had put on his Jeremiah face a number of times for the media, and tomorrow he planned to give a good bollocking to the government's Inter-Agency Working Party on Climate Change Adaptation, who had invited him for their annual Hui Taumata. Any of a hundred local scientists would have done a fine job, but they evidently wanted the cachet of an international guest star to ensure good media coverage of their big meeting.

So he was expected in Ngaruawahia tomorrow, but he'd flown over a week earlier to revisit old haunts. He'd started in Southland, where he was surprised to find Lumsden, the little town that bore him, struggling on with its wind turbines and its knick-knack shops. They still remembered him there, and remembered the small plane crash that had killed his parents. He didn't stay in Lumsden long.

For the last three days, he'd been wandering around Dunedin, watching the traditional passive aggression between students and lecturers play itself out, climbing Flagstaff and trying once more to spot the hills south of Clinton. He had left today's pilgrimage till last, but here he was, walking down Centre Road in the autumn sunshine, heading for Smaills Beach.

But why?

He stopped walking, wandered over to a fencepost, and stood staring south-west at the city while he tried to answer the question. There was something waiting for him at the beach, he felt. Something unfinished.

As he neared the bottom of the hill, where the road expired in a cluster of derelict houses, the noonday sun eluded the clouds to shine on the waters below. There was no doubt about it: the mean sea level was higher. The beach had been driven back inland, and the lowest of the old houses was almost buried beneath the dunes.

He worked his way down the lupin-covered slope and through the tough marram grass that covered the dunes, smelling the sea air, hearing the cries of gulls that might have circled above his head on the lonely Southland beaches of childhood.

When he surmounted the last line of dunes and stood on the beach itself, he felt deflated. He had wanted the waves to be angry, to roar and growl, to hurl themselves at the beach in their efforts to claw him back; but the sun shone, the surf was gentle, and the voice of the deep was the merest mutter of foam. The only inhabitant of the beach to take the slightest interest in him was a small black-and-white dog, perhaps part-spaniel, that appeared from his left, bounding along with its tail and ears flying. Even it ignored him until he picked up a stick and motioned to throw; then the dog bounced around him, running away, turning back, scrawling circles of anticipation in the sand. As he raised the stick high above his head, the dog's owner hove into view. 'Fang!' she called.

Fang hesitated for a moment, torn between the lure of the stick and the wrath of its mistress, then turned and trotted away with one last reproachful glance over its shoulder. The young woman shielded her eyes from the sun, looking at him. He waved, but she turned away, following Fang down the beach towards Tomahawk.

Martin was alone on Smaills Beach.

He started to walk towards the headland at the northern end of the beach, wondering whether the stream was still there. It was, but it now flowed out through a stop-bank that protected the fields behind. Someone — maybe the farming family that used to live here — had put a lot of work into that bank, but it had not been maintained lately, and the cracks were beginning to show. Soon the abandoned fields would become swamp and then lagoon. Mangroves would grow here for a while, until the sea rose too high even for them.

That was the news he had for the officials and the politicians, with all their 'business as usual' and their 'least-cost mitigation'. It was too late for all that. The remaining fossil fuels were still being burnt, too many hectares of forest and forest soil had gone, and emissions trading had turned out to be just an expensive shell game. The rate of temperature increase was itself increasing. Things were bad, and they were going to get much worse.

He distrusted such bald prognoses even as he made them. Nature had a way of imposing limits; there might be some self-correcting mechanism as yet undiscovered. It would have to be dramatic to have much effect; perhaps the whole West Antarctic Ice Sheet would cease to burden the weary continent and would slide off into the Southern Ocean, lowering sea temperatures and setting in motion a new ice age. Perhaps there'd be a nicely calibrated nuclear war that threw just enough dust into the atmosphere to offset the increased CO_2. Perhaps benevolent aliens were coming Earth's way at the speed of light, ready and willing to fix up the mess humanity had made of the planet.

Perhaps not. He didn't see any virtue in shading the truth. In less than a century, large areas of the earth would be unfit for human habitation. Let them set up a working party to deal with that.

He turned from the stream and started back down the beach, kicking at the driftwood. An old song circled his head, something about running. Footsteps in sand. He peered back up the hill for a moment, then stopped and turned his gaze to the sea.

As he stood there, looking south by east, the clouds that had been building since noon covered the sun once again, and soon a fine drizzle began to fall. At the other end of the beach, Fang's owner decided she'd had enough exercise for today and headed for cover.

Martin didn't notice the rain. He had stopped noticing much of anything but the rise and fall of the surf, the patient song of the waves. He stood for a full ten minutes, disconnected.

Something brushed his leg. He looked for the source of the disturbance and discovered that Fang had somehow escaped from its owner and, remembering the promise of a game, had found a stick and sought him out.

'Hello, little dog,' said Martin. 'You're keen, aren't you?'

Fang dropped the stick at his feet and stood there looking up at him. Martin picked it up and threw it high into the air; the dog lost track of it for a moment, then raced towards it as it bounced on the hard sand by the water's edge, picked the stick up, and ran back towards Martin. Fang wasn't the world's best retriever; it — or rather she, as a rear view had revealed — veered aside as Martin reached for the stick, and made quite a play of refusing to give it up. Even after she dropped the tattered twig, Fang stood over it, growling when Martin's hand strayed too close. As he seized it from beneath her muzzle, Fang was already bounding off in anticipation of another throw.

They had enacted this little ritual half a dozen times when Martin remembered why he was here. The next time he secured the stick, he did not throw it right away, but stood, looking hard at it — it might have been beech perhaps, some remnant of Gondwanaland's crumbling circumpolar forest — and at Fang's bright and eager eyes.

'Here, dog, fetch!' And he threw the stick as hard as he could out to sea. It fell somewhere in the deeper water and disappeared from view.

Martin regretted the impulse as soon as the stick left his hand. 'Come back, Fang,' he called, but the rising wind robbed his voice of power, and in any case the dog was far too set on finding the trophy and returning it so the game could continue. She was already out of her depth, and was using her best dog-paddle; but her legs were short, the waves were swift and cold, and the stick was nowhere to be seen.

'Fang! Come back, Fang! You'll drown, you stupid little mutt.' A larger wave broke over Fang's uplifted muzzle, and for a good ten seconds she was lost from view; then she reappeared, still heading out to sea.

He was dressed in a grey jacket, cable-knit jersey, and faded corduroy trousers. Not stopping to think, he stripped them off and raced out after Fang. The surf rose just as he'd remembered: calf, knee, thigh, stomach and chest. He was getting out of his depth now, just like the dog. Was that her? Yes! Afloat and whining, swimming in jerky circles three metres further out. He called her name once again, and her ears lifted in response. Turn this way, dog, turn this way — she was coming closer now, and behind her came a wave big enough to wash right over his head. How firm was his footing? Was there a hollow to his left?

He turned his back before the wave reached him, and an amalgam of panicked dog and cold southern ocean hit him squarely on the back of the neck. He was lifted off his feet and hurled in towards the shore, a surfing gooney bird. His right foot connected with a rock; he thrust a hand out and it clasped another rock, this one above sea level. He had run into one of the outriders of the headland, and was able to get his head above the waves and clamber to his feet.

And where was Fang? He looked almost all around him before discovering her bedraggled form on a ledge directly below. She offered no resistance when he hauled her up with him. 'Come on, wee dog. You're okay now. I'm sorry, I'm sorry . . .' Fang's tail wagged feebly as he stroked her head and crooned.

There was the matter of getting to safety. The headland was too steep to climb. They weren't very far away from shore, but there was no telling the depth of the water directly shoreward of the rock. What was the tide doing? The rain was getting colder — and the clothes he had left on the beach were getting damper.

'Okay, Fang. Last lap.' He cradled the shivering Fang in his arms, walked to the leeward edge of the rock, took a deep breath, and jumped.

And stubbed his toe again; there were more rocks down there. But the water was barely a metre deep, and without further misadventure Martin and the dog he had nearly killed returned to dry land.

'Two towels, dog, that's what we need. Where's your owner got to when we need her? She shouldn't let you run around by yourself. You might get into trouble.' By the time his jacket had dried them both, its value as a garment had been severely reduced. It would be a long, cold walk back up Centre Road to his car.

Fang seemed to bear Martin no ill-will; on the contrary, she trotted faithfully at his heel as he made his damp and gritty way back through the sandhills. They had almost reached Centre Road again when Fang's harassed owner came running up from the city end of the beach.

'There you are, you mongrel. Where the hell have you been? You're a bad dog. BAD DOG! And you're all wet. What have you been doing with her?'

'She came up to me with a stick, so we've been playing fetch. It was good fun, wasn't it, Fang?'

'Well, she's my bloody dog. Why is she wet?'

'Oh, I chucked one or two in the surf. She's fine, really. You go home now, Fang.'

Fang looked at Martin until it was clear that another stick would not be forthcoming, then returned to her owner, who looked her over carefully.

'She's soaked through!'

Martin shifted nervously on his feet, as if prepared for flight.

'Look, to be honest, she got in a bit deep, and I had to jump in and get her out. Keep her in front of the fire for a while. I'm really sorry. If there's any problem, call my cell — here's the number, see — I'll be there till tomorrow morning. She's a lovely dog: you're a lucky woman to have her.' He stood awkwardly, legs spread, palms uplifted in appeasement.

'If you've hurt her—'

Watching the woman cradling the shivering beast, Martin realised she must be no more than twenty-two or three. A student, maybe, the dog a reminder of life on a farm far away. She had short dark hair that framed an oval face, a trim figure, Doc Martens on her feet . . . 'Look, call me tomorrow morning, would you?' he said. 'I'd like to know she's okay.' With a final tentative wave to Fang, he turned and walked away.

He was staying with fellow academics, an Otago University professor and her husband. He tried to make conversation at dinner, but his heart wasn't in it. He made his excuses early, pleading tiredness — well, that was true enough — and went to bed a little after nine.

For a long time he could not sleep, but sleep when it did come was untroubled by the dreams of green water that had followed him around the globe. He woke some time after midnight to moonlight shining through thin curtains. He rose and opened the windows, looking out over the sloping garden and the silent city. The moon slipped among high clouds turned grey and yellow by its light. Down in the valley, a mist was gathering. If the sea broke on some lightless shore, he could not hear it. He yawned and went back to bed.

When he awoke, he felt calm, more rested than he had for fully twenty years. He did not feel the fate of the Earth, the weight of the sea, pressing down on his forehead; his only fear was for Fang.

The call came at breakfast.

'Martin Fisher here.'

'You asked me to call.'

'About Fang?'

'She's fine. She's a tough old thing. Hey, I'm sorry I got mad at you. Do you have a dog of your own?'

'No, but I'd like to, one day. Thanks for calling. Tell me, are you a student?'

'That's right.'

'What of?'

'Music. Do you play music?'

'No, I don't do that either. I haven't really had the time. Well . . .'

'Jane.'

'. . . And I'm Martin. Well, Jane, I'm flying out of Dunedin today and back to the States in a week, so we'll probably never see each other again, but will you promise me something?'

'I might . . .'

'Don't give up, will you? Never give up.'

'Are you all right?'

'Yes, I'm fine. Never give up, Jane. Goodbye.'

He switched off his phone to find the professor looking at him.

'Friend of yours?'

'A young woman I met at the beach. When we get to our age, I think we're entitled to pass on good advice. Wouldn't you say?'

The professor raised an eyebrow.

Let her think what she liked, thought Martin. He looked out the window. The sun was shining. He had a plane to catch, a meeting to attend. Perhaps he would hear something new. He stood up, suddenly eager to be on his way.

MORNING ON VOLKOV

In the yellow morning light, the bay slumbered on, as it had for millennia. The greasy wavelets that lapped against the shore were the only hint of life.

Suzanne woke first. She stretched to look out the window, peering through the heavy atmosphere at dark rock and sea. Only the most determined photons from the young sun above filtered through the cloud cover to shed their light on the bay. Today would be like yesterday and all the days before: overcast and mild.

'Laszlo!'

An undefined mumbling emerged from the pile of quilts and blankets that hid her partner. Had he always been this lazy? She didn't think so, but after two-and-a-half years on this mudball it was getting hard to remember.

'Wake up, you lazy sod. We've got to replace the filters in the monitors today, remember? Let's do it before it gets too warm.'

Another mumble. It took three good kicks to get him moving.

Although Suzanne and Laszlo found it hard to remember what they were doing there, there were good reasons for their presence on the planet. Volkov III had just one thing going for it: of all the worlds humanity had investigated in its slim segment of the galaxy, Volkov was the only one which came anywhere near duplicating the conditions thought to have prevailed on the proto-organic Earth. The land, air, and deeper ocean were barren, but complex chemicals made a tenuous soup of the shallow coastal seas. If current theory was correct, conditions were ripe for the emergence of the first fully living cells.

'Breakfast?'

'No. Not hungry.'

'Come on, Laszlo, we're going to need some energy to lug those filters around. It's bad enough already, living on this recycled crap, without you going on hunger strike.'

'Okay, okay. Pass me those tasty sludgewafers, honey.'

'What have you got in mind for dinner? The usual?'

''Fraid so, unless there's some spare protein floating around out there.'

Breakfast over, they struggled into their cumbersome atmosphere suits and cycled the airlock. The suits and the stronger gravity made movement difficult, but a few plodding steps took them down to the shore of the bay, its water leaden beneath the cloud. The monitors were located from a few metres to more than a kilometre offshore; even that far out, the water was only thigh-deep, but it was tiring to wade so far, bend down and replace the old filters — clotted as they were with proto-organic gunk — and struggle back to shore with their extra weight. The old filters then had to be cleaned and made ready for re-use. In an Earth fortnight, the new filters would become the old filters, and they'd have to go through the whole process again. Laszlo and Suzanne had been changing the filters now for two-and-a-half years, and not a damned thing had happened to break the monotony.

Well, thought Suzanne, that wasn't quite true. The measurements they took showed that the complexity of the proto-organic system in the bay was increasing; that complexity should continue to increase until the point that marked the transition from proto-life to life itself. Whether this would happen before their replacements arrived (now in just six months' time) used to be a burning question, when they could still find the energy to talk about it.

Oh, they had talked about that and everything else when they first arrived, two young graduates lured by the opportunity to see life in the making. For six months or so, they had gone about everything — work, sex, play — with wide-eyed fervour. But the weather had remained grey and warm and damp, and the computers had reported nothing dramatic, and the food tasted always the same, and their enthusiasm had ebbed away. Boredom and relaxation were dangerous, yet even the nagging risks of living on a largely unknown world became boring after a while.

Sex, books, and music had all been replayed too many times, and their favourite pastime now, on days when nothing needed fixing or changing, was to submerge in the soup and drift off to sleep. Not long after arriving, they'd taken to lying around on the shore like armoured sunbathers, watching the slow eddies of the bay and letting their suits take the burden of gravity. Suzanne had suggested they'd be even more comfortable lying in the shallows, and the suits proved just as good at coping with an amphibious life. They slept longer and more peacefully here than in the dome, yet they still seemed to need more rest each day.

Floating on the tide, changing filters, sending reports back to base, they whiled away the days. The shabby interior of the dome became less welcoming with each return. The Volkov expedition had been plagued by financial difficulties from the start; Suzanne just hoped there would be enough money to pay for the relief crew, and that they wouldn't be stuck here for another three years. Their relationship had settled into irritability on Suzanne's part matched with lethargy on Laszlo's; their professional interest in life on Volkov had been all but extinguished.

'Sheldrake,' said Suzanne. They were back in the dome, in the workshop, cleaning filters.

'What?'

'Sheldrake. Dr Rupert Sheldrake and the Hypothesis of Formative Causation. Heard of it?'

'No.'

'I prepped it at college. This Sheldrake was a well-respected botanist, or something like that, who suddenly came out with the idea that once something new happens — a new compound crystallises, say, or an animal becomes the first of its species to learn a new skill — "morphogenetic fields" are set up which make it more likely that the compound will crystallise in future or that other members of the species will learn the same skill.'

'Sounds crazy.'

'That's what most people said. Lots of critics pointed out that crystals could travel from one place to another and trigger subsequent crystallisations, and so on. He came up with answers to those points, though, and he—'

'Anyone can sound plausible. Remember McCluskey and his "alien ruins" on Triton?'

'You did History of Science too, eh? The thing was, Sheldrake proposed some experiments to test his hypothesis. For instance, teaching mice in London a new trick and carrying out a blind experiment in Los Angeles to see if mice there learnt faster once the London mice had cracked it.'

'Couldn't the mice just get from London to Los Angeles before the second experiment was done?'

'I don't know. Maybe they did the second experiment later the same day, or something. Besides, I think London and Los Angeles are quite far apart. Anyway, Sheldrake managed to persuade some wealthy businessmen to put up money to test the theory out. Various experiments were made, and Sheldrake's supporters claimed the case was proved, but the scientific establishment wasn't going to give in without a fight. Counter-experiments were run, papers presented, symposia held — you know the story. Neither side convinced the other, and since no firm conclusions were reached and most people could get along quite happily without morphogenetic fields, Sheldrake was eventually filed and pretty much forgotten.'

'Why the sudden interest in Mr Sheldrake?'

'His evidence looked pretty convincing to me. Let's suppose he was right. This planet should be just on the verge of producing life—'

'Whatever that is.'

'— whatever that is, okay, self-replicating organisms. Once it happens, according to old Rupert, it should happen more and more often as the morphogenetic effect grows stronger. There's no way of telling how long that process might take: substantial numbers of self-replicators could be produced within a few days.'

'How exciting.'

'If you weren't so bloody negative, you'd realise what that could mean. Rather than a gradual transition to life, it might happen all at once. You know, like Chaos Theory, or did you sleep through that too?'

Sheldrake's fields are subtle things, and it may be that Suzanne's sudden recollection of Sheldrake and his theory was prompted by the morphogenetic field of the self-maintaining, self-replicating organism that had just come into existence in that shallow bay. As the field strengthened, the energy barriers that had previously prevented such organisms from forming were lowered; and as the barriers lowered and more reactions led to life, so the field grew ever stronger. On Earth, the field of a new form of life would have been diluted by the fields of a thousand others, but here, on Volkov, the new field had no competition, and it called all organic matter to attain its level of complexity.

When Laszlo and Suzanne awoke the next morning, they both felt that something had changed. When they checked the readings on the computer, the difference was obvious.

'It's started!' Suzanne said. Laszlo just grimaced.

'Don't like the look of it?'

'It's not that. My stomach's upset.'

'Stay here and I'll go out to take a look.'

'You think I'm going to miss the first interesting thing that's happened since we got here?' He was already climbing into his suit, and was well out into the bay by the time Suzanne had suited up and left the airlock. She had to call him several times on the radio before he answered.

'Laszlo! What can you see?'

'Not a lot. I'm going to check further out — getting harder to move now . . .'

His voice sounded strange, as if he had bubbles in his throat. Suzanne was about to tell him to come back to shore when she saw him bend, as if to look at something. He remained doubled over for half a minute, then collapsed face forwards into the water.

'Laszlo?' No answer. Battling the viscous fluid, she tried to run to his aid.

She had waded halfway to him when the loosening began. The complex partnership of specialised cells that forms the human body had no place among the coalescing proto-life of Volkov III. The least specialised cells, those closest to their free-swimming ancestors, were first to heed the morphogenetic call. They began to detach themselves from their fellows; nuclei and other cell components remembered their independent ancestry and attempted to regain it. Tissue ruptured and dissolved, flesh melted, bone crumbled. Suzanne fell forward, the sea of her womb joining its ocean, the river of her gut flooding her torso, the stream of her thought dying in a greater flow. The ghost of a hand opened her suit, and the waters mingled. Two suits wallowed in the gentle swell, waiting for the relief team to arrive.

THE ROYAL TOUR

Señor Borges visited the region of orogeny. No mountains grow faster than those of the Southern Alps, he was told, and he felt through the bones of his feet the struggle between the rock pushing upwards and the water washing it away.

At the high-country station, lunch was followed by a sheep shearing demonstration. The smell of dung and sweat recalled vividly to his memory the estancias of his youth, the gauchos small then large against the pampas. The wool that now passed through his fingers — finest Perendale, finest Romney — was the same wool he had pressed into bales in the warm, dark shed owned by Señor Robles and his two brothers, where he had coughed and sweated his way through the summer. The trees that darkened the mountain valleys also grew in southern Argentina. New Zealand, Tasmania, Patagonia: all one, divided by ocean and time.

He was returned to Dunedin, where a civic reception supplied everything needed for sleep but a pillow. In the morning, he was escorted to the Royal Albatross colony at Taiaroa Head. The view of the Pacific Ocean was lost on him, and, even supported by the two soldiers who formed his personal guard of honour, he was consumed by the fear of falling. It was a relief to all concerned when the allotted time ended and he could leave.

En route to the nation's capital, Señor Borges rebelled. He was prepared to visit the institute of penal reform and open the motorway extension, he said, and his meeting with the Prime Minister was inevitable, but what was the point in his attending the dance performance? He was not the titular patron of the Royal New Zealand Ballet, and he would be unable to see the performance, so any praise he might offer could only bring shame to him and mortification to the performers. Let him give his apologies to the dancers and visit the National Library instead.

On this point, after much consultation with the guardians of protocol, his will prevailed.

As soon as he entered the dry air of the library, Señor Borges relaxed. The familiar scents of books and readers conducted themselves to his nose. He roamed the research collections, where the rare book librarians, fiercest guardians of the mysteries, permitted him to run his fingers over the ridged and whorled pages of Shackleton, of Cook, of Milton. He descended to the stacks in the basement.

Elsewhere in the garden of forking paths, the prince was attending the dance performance, his mouth set on

Smile as he counted down the moments until he could return to his palace and his bride. Señor Borges also smiled. He murmured to the stacks, who replied in languorous whispers. The dialogue continued until his minders led him away, and though the Prime Minister flaunted her knowledge of Argentine literature and geography throughout dinner, she could not disturb the smile that animated the old man's face.

QUEEN OF THE SNOWS

I passed Burgess at two thousand metres, halfway across the difficult traverse between Pearson Col and the Forgotten Icefall. It was clear he was struggling.

'What's wrong? Altitude sickness?'

'Briefcase too heavy.' He clasped it to himself and struggled on.

The icefall is treacherous at the best of times, but today it was rotten with seracs and consultants. I saw a respected senior counsel almost carried off when a great horn of ice crashed down on the ledge he was crossing, and was forced to waste valuable time rescuing the Manufacturers' Association from a crevasse. I barely made it back onto firm snow by nightfall, and had to pitch my tent by moonlight.

I rose to a fair dawn and lost no time in striking camp. Weather like this was too good to waste. My breath froze before me as, with crampons and ice-axe, I toiled up the slope and onto the summit ridge, my eyes dazzled by the sun and the view.

I was on the summit almost before I knew it, and there she was: her flashing eyes, her floating hair, her laptop and satellite modem.

'Name?'

'Loveridge. I'm here about—'

'Inquiry, commission, inquisition? Choose wisely.'

'We were hoping for a select committee.'

She froze me with a look. 'A Commission of Inquiry will commence on this spot in two weeks, weather permitting. All participants should be represented by counsel. Dismissed.'

'But—'

'Two weeks. Be here at dawn.'

I backed out of the Presence.

The thought of roping twenty lawyers together and shepherding them up the Forgotten Icefall was so appalling that I didn't notice Burgess toiling upwards until I was almost on top of him. He looked paler than ever.

'Got a moment?' he gasped. 'How did it go?' He sank gratefully onto the snow.

'Got what I came for. Back in two weeks.'

'What was she wearing?'

'A brown survival suit with a yellow outer jacket. A woolly hat and typing gloves. Is that enough to go on?'

'You realise that wasn't her?'

'Wasn't who?'

'You didn't meet the Queen. That was her secretary. She schedules meetings, but she doesn't make decisions. I', said Burgess proudly, 'am meeting the Queen in thirty minutes.'

'You'd better hurry, then.'

Delaying my descent wasn't wise, and I paid for it later with a frantic scramble in the half-dark; but there wasn't room to hide a postage stamp on that summit, and only one route led there. To meet Burgess, the Queen had to pass me. Shivering in the rising wind, I watched him toil upward.

He was almost at the summit when she came. Borne aloft by her red and green plumage, uttering a single harsh cry, the Queen of the Snows wheeled once in the thin cold air before settling on her mountain throne.

GOING TO THE PEOPLE

Mind if I sit down here? Thanks. Haven't seen you around here before — you're from offworld, aren't you? Been down here long — know anybody yet? Didn't think so. Tell you what: buy me a drink and I'll tell you a story, fill in a few minutes for you. It's a true story; a cautionary tale, you might say. Thank you . . . yes, that'll do fine. Your health.

So. You might not think it to look at me, but about a year ago I graduated from Felsen University — Felsen's Planet, Arcturus Sector — graduated with a degree in Social Organisation and Political Science. Good degree, too, and I was sure it was going to lead to a better job. I could have stayed behind on Felsen, working for the Sector Administration or somesuch, but I'd just broken up with my second medium-term contract and I wanted to breathe some different air for a while. She'll do well there — good career ahead of her. Sensible woman.

Anyway, I got this idea I'd put my education to practical use in politics somewhere. Not as a candidate, at least for starters, but as a campaign manager or something like that. If I'd had any sense I'd have started small — got a staff post on a major campaign in the Home Worlds, say — but I was looking for a pond where I'd be the biggest fish. I figured that might be in one of the newly colonised areas further away from Terra, seeing as how the good old Sector Admin had been working pretty damn hard to get things out there in some kind of order. Example: ever been to Mazenkis IV? Heard of it, eh? Well, fifteen standard years ago, things were pretty rough even there. They'd been having a lot of trouble collecting Federal taxes thereabouts, so the word was out from on high to tidy things up or else. As part of that process, they'd cobbled together a region based on the Kalphan system and were about to hold elections for a Regional Assembly.

That was taking tidying up too far, because some of the eleven worlds involved had barely been settled. What's more, there were two non-human species in the region: the Kalphans themselves, who dominated their home system and had a presence in the other five, and the Floort, who were confined to the single inhabitable world in their tinpot little system. I found the situation pretty intriguing, actually — three species, all oxycarbon of course but with fairly different outlooks on life . . . too bloody different! Anyway, these three species, right, but none of them knew the others all that well and here they were being shoehorned into a common administration.

Could make a name for myself here, I thought, so I took the next ship out.

I headed for Pletanar, the main human planet in the region, and when I arrived I hunted up as many of the human candidates as I could to see if they needed an expert like myself to sweep them into office. I guess most of them had enough sense to figure that I'd do them more harm than good, but just as I was thinking I'd better register with the local employment office, one of the party HQs put me in touch with their man on Floort. He turned out to be a Felsen Uni type like myself, a lawyer who'd been hauled back from Felsen to the family practice on Floort. Apparently his parents had been paying his varsity bills and wanted some work from him in return. He'd jumped at the chance to say goodbye to Floort as an assemblyman on Kalphan when it arose. As he proudly pointed out, he was a very glib young man, but he needed a master tactician behind the scenes. I said I was just what he needed, and he agreed.

There were four seats at stake there and my man, Anrac, was the only human candidate. The other three seats were out in the wops from a human point of view, and various Floort were fighting them out, but we had just the one Floort opposing us. The other human parties and the human–Kalphan alliance that was expected to win overall obviously didn't consider our electorate worth bothering about, but Anrac and I had other ideas. Still, I didn't like the way the Floort seemed united behind one candidate. The way I looked at it, although this ought to rally the humans behind Anrac it could mean inter-species strife wasn't far off, and there were more of them than us. I set out to learn all I could about the Floort, but I didn't get very far.

Pletanar had been settled by us for only thirty years. The humans had their own problems to sort out, and the natives kept themselves to themselves except for a bit of trading, so data on them was very sketchy. A Galactic Survey team had breezed through fifty years back, but at that time we were just making contact with the S'taith Confederacy and nobody had much time for a pack of talking kangaroos. Kangaroos: you must have seen pictures of them? Terran things — bounce around. Yeah, that's right. The Floort are pretty similar to look at, but intelligent. Actually, since they're nomads for most of the year on a planet with plenty of food, it's strange they're so smart. They've got a well-developed culture, language, religion, and so on, but nothing to beam home about in the way of technology, so their main trade with the humans was in food and furs. Floort's blessed with good farmland but little else, so that's what the humans did: farm, drink, fight, and screw. Fought among themselves, mind you, not much with the natives — said they could be nasty when cornered.

It wasn't really the time and place for sophisticated market research, demographic analysis, and the other stuff I'd found so absorbing back on Felsen. Our basic strategy was to promise both sides a lot and hope they didn't start comparing notes. We told the humans that they needed a voice of their own — to wit, Anrac — and that he'd protect their status as representatives of our great civilization. Not that they were very good advertisements for it. Through our translation machines, we told the Floort that we could bring them development, growth, and a new era of progress: 'a path to the stars', as our slogan for them read in Terran. Since they'd never seen the results of growth, development, progress, and the like on other worlds, and since the few of them that we did some impromptu market research on seemed to like the words, it seemed a pretty safe and maybe profitable course to steer.

The main problem we had was catching up with the damned things to deliver our spiel. They moved all over the place in their packs, and how the electoral office expected to make sure that the same Floort that were in the electorate when it was drawn up were going to be there on polling day, I'll never know. We were pinning our hopes on a high human turn-out and a low Floort one, though, so we were quite encouraged by their mobility.

While I was doing my thing behind the scenes, Anrac was performing pretty well in front of the masses. Without too much scaremongering, he'd got the humans convinced that solidarity was the answer to the looming Floort menace. They still had Anrac's parents pegged as a couple of conniving old shysters, but Anrac had them convinced he was a shining beacon of rectitude. Humans out in the backblocks reported that the Floort didn't seem too thrilled by the rather minimal campaign their candidate was mounting, so with a standard fortnight to go Anrac seemed to have things well in hand. Just to be on the safe side, I advised him to make a few forays into Floort territory, particularly as they were gathering in larger numbers than usual for some sort of festival.

One sunny morning, therefore, Anrac found himself staring out across a sea of about three thousand Floort faces, by far the largest herd of them we'd seen. The Floort candidate was also there. She spoke first. It was the first and only time I heard her, and rendered into Terran her speech seemed to consist mainly of gardening hints. I didn't get it, and by their lack of visible reaction the Floort didn't either. Anrac turned to me and grinned. 'I think we've got this one,' he said.

He strode to the microphone and started into a most impressive speech. He told them about the poverty of their present lives in comparison with the riches of the Galaxy. Then he explained how he, Anrac, would be personally responsible for transforming each and every Floort from a creature of dust and darkness into a veritable Lord of the Universe. I thought he might be overdoing it a bit, but from the agitation we could all see in the crowd they seemed to be lapping it up. After all, I reflected, he'd be off-planet after the election and could break his promises from a safe distance. Encouraged by their excitement, Anrac seemed to swell as he reached the climax of his speech. Abandoning his lectern, he stepped forward to the front of the stage, flung his arms in the air, and roared, 'I give you — a new tomorrow!'

At that moment, the commotion in the crowd peaked,

the natives erupted in some kind of chant, and before any of us could move, two of them bounded onto the stage and caught Anrac by his arms. Thinking they were supporters come to congratulate him, he drew them close and bent to speak to one. The other raised its free arm, extended its claws, and slashed downwards. A line of blood stood out on Anrac's neck, then spurted skywards as he crumpled forward into the crowd. Still chanting, they bore the body off with them as the arena quickly cleared.

I sat stunned. It had happened so quickly I could barely take it in. When I finally managed to accept what I'd just seen, my overriding emotion was anger. Anger at the Floort, anger that all my good work had been undone in such an inexplicable manner. When I noticed the Floort candidate slowly hopping across the stage towards me, I wasn't sure whether to attack or to run. She stopped short of me, though, and began to explain.

'I didn't make them kill him, if that's what you're thinking. All I told them was that I would seek out new methods of growing crops and bring them back to our people. It was all that was . . . appropriate to the occasion. Surely you knew it was one of the great religious festivals of our people? At these times, we gather together to await and celebrate the appearance among us of visionaries, of people with new insights; these insights seem to emerge whenever large numbers of we Floort are gathered together. We celebrate these people, and we draw strength from them.

'Your Anrac, with his revelations of hope and change,

appeared to those celebrating this festival to be a great prophet. I have seen you work and I know that this Anrac was a liar and of little worth, but my people took him at his word. We celebrate our prophets, Mr Genarth, and we draw on them. If the vision is great then the draw must also be great, to restore the balance of our shared existence. We Floort are omnivores like you humans, and sometimes we draw our sustenance from blood . . .'

I know that little speech off by heart now. I've played our tape of it back several times, trying to figure out where I went wrong. Anyway, I got off that planet as fast as I could after we'd gone through all the necessary formalities. I got as far as this spaceport, which is where my . . . ah . . . severance pay ran out. I guess I'd better get myself back together and get a job, eh? Maybe there's an election campaign on here somewhere? Hey, that's an idea — after all, I can point out that my last candidate received overwhelming support! No, I mean it: profit from your mistakes, that's what I say. Thanks for the drink and the chat, mate; I think it's put me back on the right track. Ta-ra!

COLD STORAGE

People want to believe. People want to believe that somebody cares, that love conquers all, that he meant it when he said he'd phone, that the Abdominator will tighten up that flabby tummy — now!, that it's all a giant conspiracy, that Elvis lives, or died to save our souls.

People want to believe that hideous beings from nightmare dimensions once ruled our Earth and are scheming to get it back. I was told this six months from the end of my minimum four-year sentence for insurance fraud. (Ever heard of Standard Insurance of Nebraska? No? Well, now you know why.) I had just about had enough of stuffing mailers for the day (today it was the Ellen for President PAC who were taking advantage of the competitive rates offered by our privatised prison) when I got the word I was wanted in the Team Leader's office.

Team Leader Whitley was sitting behind his desk like

a man who'd felt a lot happier when everyone had to call him 'Warden'. Beside him stood two Feds. 'Sit down, Cusack,' said Whitley. 'These boys from Washington want to have a word with you.' And he left.

The Feds kept standing. I kept sitting.

I'm not good with silence. 'Somebody died, boys?' I asked.

Travis — Fed. No. 1— came around the desk fast. He did that thing where they tip your chair back and trap you in it. 'Over to you, Cliff,' he said.

And Cliff had quite a story to tell. The two of them had been assigned to a bizarre series of burglaries: rare book and manuscript collections at universities and private colleges throughout the north-east had been ransacked. In Providence, RI, a librarian who disturbed the thieves had paid with her life. The thefts and the murder had stirred up certain influential members of the academic community, who were convinced that they were part of some wider plot. They'd managed to get the FBI interested, and now Travis and Cliff were trying to get a handle on the case.

Cliff paused for breath around about then, and I asked, in the nicest possible way, what the hell this had to do with me. Travis tipped my chair forward, hard, so my head banged on Whitley's desk. I protested. Cliff told me not to take it personally and kept right on talking.

'Our usual methods weren't working in this case, so we decided we need something to flush the perpetrators out. We think they're looking for a manuscript that doesn't exist — but if it does, it has some dangerous secrets in it.

So we've decided you're going to sell it to them.'

'Bad luck, guys. I had it, but I ate the last page yesterday.'

'Shut up, you stupid little jerk, and listen. Right now, our labs are putting the finishing touches to that manuscript. We put a few things in there that should bring the case to a satisfactory conclusion.'

'Okay. I've got two questions. Why can't your boys sell it to them? And why should I cooperate with you when I'm out of here in six months?'

Cliff nodded to Travis. Travis let go of my neck, let the chair down on the floor, and picked up the story.

'The folks at Quantico are better at some things than others. Brave, tenacious, brilliant, for sure, but they're not too good at *pretending*. We hear you are. You're the best there is — well, the best we've caught.'

I was flattered.

'And if you don't cooperate, we'll tell the state authorities about the body of that small-time operative who turned up in the East River just after the Macy's sting went wrong. Think you can talk your way out of that one? Of course, if you do cooperate we'll pay you. You'll be Special Agent Randy Cusack for the duration of this one. On full pay and benefits. Just give us your Swiss account number.'

'Sounds reasonable so far. One more question: what is this so-called manuscript about?'

'Raising the dead. But don't try it on the Macy's guy.'

Six weeks later, I was in a helicopter, heading for a private yacht moored off the Big Island of Hawaii. I was Geoffrey de Montfort, antiquarian and rare book dealer, descended on my father's side from the French de Montforts, and on my mother's from English settler stock that went right back to the *Mayflower*, intermixed (so it was whispered) with an illicit tincture of Penobscot Indian. I had no living relatives. I had been married once, to a showgirl I had met on a rare trip to New York; but there had been no true meeting of minds, and the marriage had not lasted. The young woman had been killed in an automobile accident not long after our divorce, and there had been no issue. I was prematurely grey, a little stooped, a keeper of diaries, a quiet man with only one real passion: books.

In other words, they had made me into a complete asshole. I couldn't stand Geoffrey de Montfort, and the sooner this job was over, the better.

On top of all the de Montfort crap, they had filled my head with the most incredible load of superstition, fact, and fiction that together went by the name of the 'Cthulhu Mythos'. A wacko called Lovecraft from Providence began it all, and since then a bunch of other hacks and scribblers had been adding to Lovecraft's basic outline. Now there was an immense number of stories, poems and novels, all about a bunch of anatomically unlikely beings of great antiquity who had kicked Earth around like a beach ball until they packed up and left for spring break. With the right mystical mumbo-jumbo, you could still whistle them up and get them to do your bidding — or so the Mythos claimed.

Which was really no problem, since it was all fiction, right? But Travis and Cliff had come to the conclusion that there was someone — a rich, powerful someone — who didn't think it was fiction at all, and was trying to turn it into fact. And here was I, Geoffrey de Montfort, about to give that someone what he or she was looking for.

The FBI boys set me up in a bookshop — me, in a bookshop! — and let out the word that I had a handle on this manuscript. Then we waited for the fish to take the bait. Three days ago, he did, and now we were about to meet.

The helicopter set down on the afterdeck of a floating palace. I got out in my slow, uncertain, Geoffrey de Montfort-ish way, and tottered over to shake the hand of the tanned, smiling man who advanced to greet me. He looked like a Hollywood lawyer, but cosmetic surgery can do that for anyone.

'Welcome to the good ship *Tekeli-Li*, Mr de Montfort. I hope you'll have a pleasant and rewarding stay.'

'I hope so too, Mr . . . ?'

'Oh, just call me Ed. We're all on first-name terms here.'

'Now, about the—'

'Now, now, Geoff — can I call you Geoff? — let's not talk business just yet. Isn't it a glorious day?'

I had to admit he was right. The sunlight sparkled off the wavetops, the clouds floated on the breeze, and I wouldn't have been surprised if a school of fish had jumped out of the water and waved their fins at me.

'Very attractive, Ed. I believe you have a cabin ready for me?'

'Sure, sure. Right this way.' With one well-tanned arm about my shoulders, he led me to my stateroom.

I was pretty sure the stateroom would be bugged, so I didn't remove any of the nifty FBI gadgets from their various uncomfortable hidey-holes (Geoffrey de Montfort walked with a very upright posture). Instead, I de-Montforted my way around, falling over things, dropping little white pills all over the bathroom floor. I was removing Geoff's summer wardrobe from my valise and arraying it in neat little piles on the King-Henry-VIII-sized bed when the manservant arrived to tell me that dinner was served.

There were four of us at dinner, not counting the silent, efficient servitors. Besides Ed and I, there was a young English woman called Melissa and an older man who was introduced as 'the Reverend'. We worked through the prawns, the lobsters, and a dessert that seemed to have started life as a pineapple, all without more than small talk. Then the coffee came, and Ed got down to business.

'Melissa, there'll be time for more tales of the Amazon tomorrow. I understand, Geoff, you have something we have all been looking for?'

'Well, I . . . that is to say, I know where it is and I have the means of obtaining it, yes.'

'And could you describe it to us?'

'The manuscript is of 64 leaves, unbound, written upon a parchment which — well, I believe it to be human skin, dried and cured.' I saw the Reverend nod gloomily at that.

'Each leaf is the length of a man's forearm from wrist to elbow, and what is to be read there is written in black ink. There are many marginal illustrations and interlineations. Some pages are rendered partially or completely illegible by water and fire damage.'

'How much?' asked the Reverend. 'How much of the thing is destroyed?'

'I would estimate less than ten percent.'

'And—' said the Rev, over what I thought was a warning glance from Ed, '— have you read it? What does it say?'

'I have some knowledge of medieval Latin, sir, but I have not read more than the first two pages. What I did read left me with a . . . disquieting impression, so that I did not wish to continue.'

More nodding heads. Ed ordered up another round of coffees and the discussion circled away from the topic again. It was Melissa the explorer — slim, athletic, and muscular, and how I wished the FBI had made me into Indiana Jones rather than Geoff the Dweeb — who brought it back to the point.

'I think we're all reasonably convinced that you've got what Ed is looking for, Geoff. The question is: where is it?'

I held up a protesting hand. 'My dear young lady, surely you don't expect me to tell you that without some arrangement as to remuneration?'

To my surprise, Ed agreed with me. He took me off to a side room, and we haggled. Geoffrey was quite good at that, and in the end we came up with a deal of half up front, half on delivery. If I could hang on to even the first half, that, plus the FBI's contribution, was going to make me a very wealthy man. Possibly a very wealthy dead man, but wealthy nevertheless.

By the time I'd checked that the first half of the money was in my bank, it had gotten late, and the party had moved to the afterdeck. Ed and the Reverend were in animated conversation, which broke off when I appeared. Melissa rose from the sea like Venus with a spear gun and climbed a ladder to join us.

'Is everything in order, Geoff?'

'Indeed it is.'

'And?'

'I have taken the liberty of contacting my associates. They are bringing me the manuscript from a location I prefer not to disclose. I shall go ashore tomorrow morning to meet them and take possession of it. When I have it, I shall call you and arrange a meeting at which the manuscript, and the balance of the funds, may be transferred.'

My associates, of course, were Travis and Cliff, plus a couple of local FBI heavies. We had chosen a clearing in the tropical jungle for the transfer, and there were five of us good guys to go up against Ed, the Reverend, and Melissa. It seemed like a reasonable match.

It wasn't. We did everything the time-honoured way: me and my minions on one side, Ed and his on the other. I walked towards Ed bearing the manuscript, he walked towards me bearing the money — just like the scene in one of those old Cold War thrillers when the prisoners are being exchanged through Checkpoint Charlie, and as daring Brit spy Sir Timothy Hyphen-Hyphen walks from East to West and sinister Soviet masterspy Velimir Grushnikov walks from West to East, they resolutely fail to look one another in the eye.

The thing about those scenes is, they usually end with gunshots ringing out from one or both sides and a close-up of blood staining the snow as the end credits roll. Maybe it was the lack of snow that put me off my guard. Whatever, as soon as I got within arm's reach of Ed, he said one word, there was a blinding flash (I know it's a cliché, but it was minutes before I could see clearly), and by the time I had come to my senses I was being hustled out of the clearing and towards a waiting van. A quick backward glance confirmed that Travis, Cliff and their friends had come off much, much worse than I had. Ed's minions frogmarched me back to Ed's black van, shot me up with some drug, and as I slid into unconsciousness I reflected that it was a man's life in the modern book trade.

When I woke up, I didn't know whether it was day or night. My head was aching, my body was shaking, and the air was throbbing. For a moment, I thought I was back in my favourite nightclub — but that had never featured Ed and the Reverend, and there they were, sitting just above me, wrapped up in furs and wearing heavy boots. I turned my head and saw Melissa, wrapped up likewise. Even she couldn't have got into the club in that outfit.

'Where are we?' I enquired groggily.

'Welcome back to the land of the living,' Ed shouted over the noise. 'Take a look out the window and you'll see.'

I saw plenty. One, that we were in a plane, and the mighty noise was coming from its propellers. Two, that we were flying above the sea. And three, that the sea was lousy with icebergs.

'Russia? Greenland?'

'Antarctica.'

And before you could say 'But I'm just a humble antiquarian bookseller,' we were making our approach run to McMurdo Base.

McMurdo turned out to be a little slice of the U.S. of A. at 78 South, complete with pecan pie and *Baywatch Nights* on DVD. Ed was on easy terms with everyone, particularly the base commander, and the Reverend, Melissa and I were taken on trust as part of his entourage. I had a story I wanted quite badly to tell, but Ed was such a hit here it seemed wiser to say nothing.

It soon became apparent that, for public consumption, we were a small, privately funded expedition investigating the Dry Valleys of Antarctica.

Ever wanted to go to the Moon or Mars? Save yourself the trouble and go to the Dry Valleys instead. For all its snow, Antarctica is actually the driest continent on Earth. Most of those blizzards are just a few snowflakes blowing from one God-forsaken part of the polar plateau to another. And there are some parts so dry that any snow that falls sublimes right back into the atmosphere, so all you get is a wilderness of rocks and stones with the odd sand dune thrown in for good measure. It looks like those old Mars Rover photos with the red bleached out.

All this information about Antarctica came courtesy of Trevor, our guide and driver. We were being flown from McMurdo to the Wright Valley. The Dry Valleys were in the part of Antarctica claimed by New Zealand, and Trevor (love that name) would drive us to our destination in a New Zealand Sno-Cat. I listened closely to 'Trev' but I struggled to understand what he was saying. New Zealanders talk funny.

When we flew down the course of a river and landed near the lake it emptied into, I didn't say 'What do you mean — Dry Valleys?', I just got my pack and stepped out into the bitter cold. Summertime in Antarctica, and the living was easy.

We bundled our gear into the waiting Sno-Cat. Trevor delayed our departure to show us the mummified body of a seal, its flesh slowly flaying away in the wind. 'They get confused and crawl inland from the sea ice,' he said. 'They can make it fifty kilometres before they die. This one's been here' — he looked at the carcass with a practised eye — 'oh, about five hundred years.'

If the valley looked desolate from the air, that was nothing to how it looked at ground level. The lake didn't help — it was frozen over apart from a narrow rim of cold, clear water, and the wind whipped little eddies of dust and ice across its surface.

'It's been growing,' Trevor said. 'We used to have a

station here, but we had to move out before we drowned. Global warming, you see.'

Trevor rattled on about maximum inflows and rivers that only flowed in summer and density structures, but I'd stopped listening by then. Instead, I studied the faces of my captors. The Reverend sat silently, worrying a fingernail and then getting out his Bible for reassurance. He didn't look like the explorer type. Melissa had been first out of the plane, had lugged more equipment than anyone else into the Sno-Cat, and was now looking around with puppy-like eagerness. All this Cthulhu stuff was probably of no interest to her — she just wanted to go places. And Ed? Ed sat there, relaxed, confident, powerful, the sort of man I had always wanted to be. I was sure that, if it suited him, he'd leave us all behind in this wilderness to freeze like the seals.

As far as Trevor knew, we were a geological expedition with connections to the University of Hawaii. The Hawaii cover provided a neat explanation of why all of us except Melissa were shivering, while Trevor, in his checked shirt with the sleeves rolled up, might have been going for a Sunday afternoon drive in his home town. A long drive: the Sno-Cat rumbled on up the valley, which was now beginning to narrow — Trevor said we were drawing close to its head, and that the great polar ice cap was just behind the rim of hills that surrounded us. Ed was now scanning the territory outside with noticeable eagerness. At last, he lifted his hand. 'We stop here,' he said.

The next few hours were spent in hard and largely silent labour, setting up our camp under Trevor and Melissa's guidance. Before Trevor left, he gave us three important reminders.

'First. You've got your radio. Don't be afraid to use it. Second. Never travel alone. And third. It may be bloody cold here, but this valley is sheltered. Whatever you do, don't try to climb up onto the ice cap. You'd be frozen in an hour. If I don't hear otherwise, I'll be back for you in two days' time. Good luck.' And with that, he climbed back into his heated cab, revved up the motor, and departed.

'Good,' said Ed. 'No time to waste. Let's get on with it. You know what we have to do.'

'I don't,' I said bravely.

'Oh, you'll find out when the time comes,' said Ed.

Well, that sounded too good to miss, so I trudged off after them. After all, I had no place else to go.

While we're trudging, let me tell you about the cold. It was late in the Antarctic summer, and because the rocks and gravel of the valley absorbed more heat than the Antarctic ice, it was actually five degrees warmer on average here than at McMurdo — according to Trevor. But it was still cold. The chill seeped up from the ground through the soles of our boots. It froze our eyelashes together behind our polarised goggles and loosened our teeth in their sockets. No matter how many layers of fur and thermal underwear we wore, it crawled in next to our skin. And that was when the air was still. When the wind blew, it felt as though knives sliced our faces.

Nevertheless, we soon found that we sweated like pigs under the bulky garments as we walked, only to have the sweat freeze on our bodies when we stopped. I suggested to Ed we should have stayed in Hawaii, but he wasn't listening.

After half an hour, we came to a pond, a shallow, brownish pool surrounded by rocks covered in a white coating. 'The white stuff is Antarcticite,' said Melissa, 'solid calcium chloride. This is Don Juan Pond, the only place in the world where it's cold enough and the air's dry enough for Antarcticite to form.'

Ed looked at her in surprise. 'You know a lot about it.'

She shrugged. 'When I knew where we were going, I did some reading. This is the saltiest body of water on Earth, so salty it never freezes right to the bottom, even at minus fifty degrees Celsius in the winter.'

'Yes,' said Ed. 'A lot of salt.' And he stared across the unruffled surface of the pool for some time, his expression unreadable.

'Some of us are getting cold here,' I reminded him after five minutes of this. Ed shook himself like a dog emerging from the water and nodded. 'Yes. Well, the sun won't be setting, but it's still getting late, and we should take a good night's rest before doing what must be done — eager though I am to see the conclusion of our labours.'

And we turned and trudged back to camp again. Another day, another dollar, I guess.

We had two two-person tents, which meant someone was going to get to sleep with Melissa. Randy Cusack, con artist and bon vivant, would have swept her into his sleeping bag in no time — or so he liked to think — but I wasn't certain yet whether the de Montfort cover had been blown, and Geoffrey de Montfort wasn't known for his way with women.

Which is probably what clinched the deal: as soon as the subject of who slept with whom came up, Melissa said, 'Geoff and I can share a tent — he won't mind,' and neither Ed nor the Reverend cared to dispute this. Perhaps they wanted to spend the night talking about salt.

When we'd both snuggled into our sleeping bags, still clad in a goodly proportion of our winter clothing, I asked her, diffidently, why we were here. She looked at me for a while before answering.

'That manuscript you obtained for us is the missing piece of a puzzle, Geoff. The last missing piece. Ed has been assembling this puzzle for the best part of twenty years. It started with a chance reference he read in a book, and now it's led us here.'

'To do what?'

'In 1931, the Nathaniel Derby Pickman Foundation financed a Miskatonic University geological expedition to explore the region inland from the Trans-Antarctic Mountains, whose foothills surround this valley. The expedition made considerable progress for a time, but then reports from it became fragmentary and contradictory. Many of the party were—'

'Great lecture,' I interjected.

'Shut up! I memorised this stuff specially. If you keep interrupting, I'll forget.'

'Sorry.'

Transported

'Good. Many of the party were killed by what was described as a freak windstorm. The survivors of that expedition were always curiously reticent about what transpired during its last days, although they made a concerted and ultimately successful attempt to prevent the departure of the planned Starkweather–Moore expedition to the same area some twenty years later.

'The Reverend told me that Ed read the official accounts of this expedition while he himself was a student at Miskatonic University. They piqued his interest, and as he made his way in the business world he devoted a part of his time and fortune to gathering further information. Three years ago, those investigations led him to mount his first Antarctic expedition. What he discovered then led him to scour the world for the manuscript you eventually found for him. You may have noticed, Geoff, that Ed is a man who gets what he wants.'

'Including you?'

She did not look offended. 'He doesn't want me for my body, Geoff, if that's what you mean — indeed, he seems completely indifferent to me. He needed someone with cold-climate experience, and I was recommended. I accompanied him on his last expedition, although he insisted on completing the final stage of it by himself. Still, with him, I've been places I never thought I'd go.'

'And the Reverend?'

'He's a strange one, isn't he? I'm never quite sure whether he loves Ed or hates him. He's known Ed for much longer than I have. He gets terribly agitated at some of the things Ed talks about, but he won't stop dogging his footsteps, and Ed seems to find him . . . useful to have around. Ed judges everyone by how much use they are to him.'

'How much use am I?'

'I'm sure you'll find out tomorrow. But I think we both need our sleep.'

Silence for a while. 'I'm not indifferent,' I said.

'Hmmm?'

'To your body. I'm not indifferent to your body.'

'I never thought you were. But let's see how things stand after tomorrow, shall we?' And with that she was silent.

The alarm told me I'd been woken up too early. We added layers of clothing, breakfasted, and trudged off again. Same path, same cold, same pond. When we got there, Ed bade us walk round its white-encrusted shore until we stood on its up-valley side.

'Over three hundred years ago,' he declaimed, 'the philosopher and sage Borellus established that a human or animal could be reconstituted after death from its essential salts. Today, we will put this to the test for quite a different order of creature.

'Many years ago, while still a student, I learned from the Reverend here of his researches into the confused notes and secret autobiography of John Charles Danforth, a junior member of the 1931 Miskatonic University Antarctic expedition — the expedition whose official records I had read in a seldom-opened crypt beneath the library of that same university. On this historic occasion, Reverend, I think it's incumbent on you to take up the story.'

The Reverend looked surprised, then took a deep breath and prepared to speak. I shivered: it wasn't warm out here. Were we in for a sermon?

'Thank you, Edward. Some of the . . . junior members of our little party may not be aware that, while still an ordained member of the Church, I became interested in certain matters about which the Church had chosen to remain silent for some hundreds of years. I discovered, in the course of lengthy researches, that what we think of as history is in reality only the topmost layer or stratum of the history of intelligent life on this planet, and that our achievements are as dust beside those of our predecessors — the race known as the Great Old Ones, the race whose final fastness and stronghold was in this hellish waste of ice and snow. Even before I heard the name of John Charles Danforth, I had reached these conclusions; and what I could decipher from his notes, shot through as they were with madness and terror, convinced me that as recently as our own century, some remnant of these beings could still be found here.

'What a civilisation they raised, in those long years before a puny, aggressive ape first came down from the trees and shook its fist at the stars! Their great cities were masterpieces of art and culture; their thought spanned the galaxies; their learning put the greatest of our scientists and mystics to shame. As I learned more of them, I found that I could no longer accept the narrow certainties of the Church in which I had been raised, and I left my pastoral duties to pursue my researches full-time.

'In the course of those researches, I encountered Edward, and he provided the encouragement and financial support I needed. His reasons, no doubt, are his own. Many of the uncanny geographical features that Danforth describes have never been found by subsequent explorers — who knows what strange distortions of time and space may have been experienced by those final survivors of the Miskatonic expedition? However, when I heard of the researches of Borellus, Danforth's mention of "the pond of salts, where the One suspended waits" became suggestive; a chance reference in a book of Antarctic geology told me what the "pond of salts" might be, and it then remained only to acquire the manuscript so expertly provided by our friend Mr de Montfort, which—'

'Was it necessary to acquire Mr de Montfort as well?' I interrupted.

Ed moved closer to me and took my arm. 'We do regret that necessity, Geoff, but we're sure that you'll find what we're about to do of interest. We believe that the salts of a Great Old One lie suspended in this pond, waiting for one who has suitable knowledge to restore it to life — not only life, but full possession of its powers, and of the secrets of the aeons! Normally, the salts would need to be dried, but the concentration of this pond is such that all that we require is the correct mixture of chemicals.

Reverend, if you please?'

The Reverend drew from his voluminous pockets an ancient phial, unstoppered it, and sprinkled its contents on the water. Nothing happened.

He and Ed looked at each other. 'I fear that an additional ingredient will be required,' said the Reverend sadly. Ed whipped out a knife and held it to my throat.

I had the time it would take him to say 'blood' to act. I jack-knifed backwards and kicked Ed in the face. The knife fell from his grasp and skittered off the rocks into the water. We both reached for it, but he was faster. That was his undoing. He plunged his ungloved hand into the pond, then screamed as the water, strong as battery acid, burnt his flesh. Before he regained his feet, I banged his head, hard, against a rock. Ed slumped into the water, a thin trickle of blood from the cut on his forehead staining it red. By the time Melissa and the Reverend pulled him out feet-first, his face was hideously disfigured. He sobbed, slobbered and whimpered.

'You've destroyed him!' cried the Reverend. Melissa just looked at me. I shrugged. 'He destroyed himself. My name is Randy Cusack, and I'm a con-man, a thief, and a murderer. So what do I care?'

'We've got to get him back to civilisation,' said the Reverend.

I considered this. 'Yeah, I suppose we have. Wipe that stuff off his face first.'

All this drama had distracted us from the pool itself. It was the sucking, gurgling noise that caught our attention.

The Reverend's researches had not been in vain, because something was rising from the water. If this was a Great Old One, I was mighty glad I hadn't been around when they ruled the planet. It had a tubular, ill-defined body with a mass of protoplasmic extrusions that shifted and writhed as it hauled itself from the rapidly shrinking pond. A cluster of tentacles surrounded its head, for want of a better word. That head rose high for a moment, seemed to sniff the air, and then pointed straight at us. The thing was coming closer.

'My God,' said the Reverend. 'That's no Great Old One! We've raised a Shoggoth!' And, his concern for Ed forgotten, he ran.

I stood rooted to the spot and watched the monstrosity approach. It was Melissa who roused me, taking my arm and screaming 'Run!' So we ran around the pond and back down the valley toward the camp, following the Reverend. We would have had no chance if the thing hadn't stopped to dispose of Ed first; we heard a brief, horrible scream, soon cut off, and then appalling sounds of sucking and slurping. My education in the finer points of criminal life sure hadn't prepared me for this.

Melissa was fit, and I had the desperation of a cornered rat. We soon caught up to the Reverend, who was tiring badly. We tried to drag him along with us, but that only slowed us all down. So we left him behind.

Hey, I never said I was a hero.

We left him, but he returned to us soon enough. We heard a shriek, and then the Reverend's body, minus its head, flew through the air and landed just in front of us. The sight was so unexpected that for a moment we stopped. In that moment, the great black bulk of the Shoggoth slid smoothly between us.

For a moment, before I screamed and ran, I caught the thing's eye. There was an intelligence there, a nightmarish awareness of my presence. The Shoggoth was thinking, considering its options: which tasty morsel to eat first?

It must have liked the taste of the Reverend's head, because it decided to eat the rest of him. So I ran once more, trying to catch up with Melissa, who hadn't stayed around to peer into the thing's soul.

As we crested a shallow hill, we could hear the Shoggoth slithering close behind — and then we could see Trevor and his Sno-Cat coming towards us. I didn't know whether a Sno-Cat could outrun the thing, but I had a keen interest in finding out.

Trevor was brave. As soon as he saw our plight he accelerated straight toward us. 'Do it!' Melissa screamed.

Do it?

Trevor jumped down from the cabin, ignored us as we ran past him, and opened his mouth. I don't know what strange language he was speaking, but whatever it was, it sure worked. The Shoggoth stopped its advance. Trevor pointed, and it circled us. He pointed again, and it wriggled its sinuous bulk onto a long trailer that the Sno-Cat was towing, then submitted as Trevor hauled a tarpaulin over it and tied it down. I was so astonished by this performance that I didn't realise Melissa was pointing a gun at me until she told me so herself.

Trevor came back and hugged her. 'Any trouble?'

'Not really. The other two are dead. It never quite got to the stage that I had to try the secondary incantations, or push Geoff in its path. What should we do with him?'

'Oh, leave him here. It's too dangerous to wake the Shoggoth to kill him, and bullets lead to questions. Geoff—'

'Randy.'

'How American. Well, Randy, I suggest you head back to the camp. You can stay warm there for a while, and the food will last for . . . maybe a week? When it's all used up, just walk out into the cold. You won't feel a thing when the end comes, and by then we'll be too far away—'

'And too rich!' put in Melissa.

'And too rich to care. Bye-bye, Randy. We've got a cargo to deliver.'

They climbed into the cabin of the Sno-Cat — Melissa still aiming the gun at me — turned, and drove off. I thought about jumping on the trailer as its tail swept by me, but I realised I would rather die than face the Shoggoth again.

But that gave me an idea. If a Shoggoth could lie suspended in that pond, why couldn't I? I went back to the camp and found the whisky. Before setting out to drink myself into enough of a stupor that I could face jumping into the pond, I decided to finish writing up this diary. If you're the one who finds it, there's a bunch of incantations jotted down at the back. Try to pronounce them just like they're written. And have some food ready. When I get out of there, I'm going to be ravenous.

BOOKS IN THE TREES

As soon as I understood what a book was, I resolved to become a bookkeeper. To the dismay of my parents, I was forever climbing trees in hopes of catching an unwary volume. Of course, I never did; they were far above me, flapping unmolested from branch to branch.

My proudest achievement was to bear back to the ground a whole egg, but my pride turned to dismay when my mother scolded me and insisted that I put it back in the nest immediately. 'That might be another Calvino or Bulgakov!' she told me. I had no idea what she was talking about, but I made the long climb anyway. (I have a strong suspicion the egg hatched into one of the flock of self-help books that used to stoop upon us as we walked, tangling their claws in our hair.)

It was not until I began my training that I realised how much more was required than the ability to climb trees.

There were cliffs, mountains, and sea-stacks to be scaled, of course, but also the myriad arts of classification and cataloguing, acquisition and disposition. The reward for endless hours of drudgery was the swoop of a thriller from a clear blue sky, the heavy 'whump' of a fantasy series flying north for the summer, the chirping of young pamphlets in the spring.

I have grown old in the service of these magnificent creatures, but I prepare for my retirement in growing dismay. The age of the book is ending. The wide forests are no more, cut down for wood and land and greed, and the great flocks of books that filled the skies of my youth have dwindled to lone volumes fleeing the hunters. Now all kinds of buzzing, brightly coloured things clamour for our attention, and books are almost forgotten.

In an attempt — perhaps it will prove vain — to preserve what we can, we have trapped many endangered books and placed them in sanctuaries we call 'libraries'. It breaks my heart to see them trammelled so; yet perhaps I shall live to see the day when booklets bred in these libraries are released back into the wild. May the last sound I hear be the rustle of their leaves.